A MILLEDUFLEUR ROSE NOVEL

RENDEZVOUS IN BRUSSELS

BOOK THREE

JAY MORONEY

RENDEZVOUS IN BRUSSELS
BOOK THREE

This is a work of fiction. All of the characters, names, incidents, organizations, and dialogue in this novel are either the products of the author's imagination or are used fictitiously.

iUniverse books may be ordered through booksellers or by contacting:

iUniverse LLC
1663 Liberty Drive
Bloomington, IN 47403
www.iuniverse.com
1-800-Authors (1-800-288-4677)

Because of the dynamic nature of the Internet, any web addresses or links contained in this book may have changed since publication and may no longer be valid. The views expressed in this work are solely those of the author and do not necessarily reflect the views of the publisher, and the publisher hereby disclaims any responsibility for them.

Any people depicted in stock imagery provided by Thinkstock are models, and such images are being used for illustrative purposes only. Certain stock imagery © Thinkstock.

ISBN: 978-1-4917-3649-4 (sc)
ISBN: 978-1-4917-3650-0 (e)

Library of Congress Control Number: 2014909943

Printed in the United States of America.

iUniverse rev. date: 05/29/2014

CHAPTER 1

Kim David was more than pleased with the recruitment of Milledufleur Rose. He and the Mossad had had her in their sights for years. Kim thoroughly reviewed the extensive file the Mossad had compiled on her. It didn't come close to describing the sheer force of her beauty and magnetism. Kim joined the Mossad shortly after it was founded. His aristocratic bearing and refined good looks were the assets that made him a natural in what became his specialty with the Mossad—recruitment of agents, especially female agents. The Mossad had learned early on about the enhanced value of their female agents. David was the best recruiter the agency had—he was, in fact, a living legend.

He used all of his many assets to recruit women as spies. He had made it a cardinal rule to not allow emotion to enter into the relationships he necessarily had to form with his recruits. This didn't interfere with his use of sex in order to achieve the agency's objectives. This didn't prevent him from the natural enjoyment from such relationships, but, for him, it was just part of the job. Since he had finished his last job several days ahead of schedule, he would use the time to make a side trip to Amsterdam before he travelled to Morocco, as he told his chief and the head of the Mossad, Hofi. Morocco was becoming less than a desirable visit. He could never abandon the mission in Morocco, but it was taking its toll on him.

He checked out of the Connaught and took a cab to Heathrow. Even after a hot shower, her aroma pervaded his space. It was more than just her aroma that pervaded his space. It was her. This encounter was more, much more than he had ever experienced. He couldn't stop thinking about her. He was becoming aware of the growing attraction and the danger it could bring to his mission. As the short flight from London was approaching Schiphol, he reluctantly concluded that he would have to see her another time. He would have to see her soon, very soon. His meeting with Hans Benson was at 1:30, and Kim suspected it would entail lunch and other activities. Benson was a freeloader of note. Benson was Managing Director of Friepoort, a distributor of minerals, chemicals, and raw materials mostly from Asia, mainly China. At their Maastricht plant, they also processed these materials for sale in Europe and in the Middle East.

David enjoyed Amsterdam—its size, convenience, and restaurants. He usually stayed at the Krasnapolsky on Dam Square. While he liked Amsterdam, he didn't like Hans Benson. Benson was a ruthless operator and a Palestinian who had immigrated to the Netherlands in the late 60s. Benson's name was Saliba, which he changed to Hans after his arrival in Holland. It was time for David to update his file on Benson's Palestinian connections. David posed as a British national who operated in North Africa, principally in Morocco as an agent of local firms. Benson had never transacted business with David, but he loved the exchange of information and David's expense account. David and the Mossad wanted to know who the Palestinians were buying their munitions from and their current channels of distribution. Disrupting this supply would save Israeli lives.

Benson had several weaknesses—prostitutes were a principal weakness that David would pay for and supply for a not-so-subtle exchange of information. He estimated that, following a very liquid lunch with Benson, he would take him to one of his favorite red light houses, but not before he had pried out of him the information they wanted. Kim would foot the bill for the women and a night at the Krasnapolsky. Benson welcomed the opportunity to escape from Maastricht and his wife on someone else's dime.

Kim's business with Benson concluded at 6. He went back to the hotel and had a good soak. He had an early flight to Morocco, so an early evening suited him. He poured himself a large whiskey and pondered the wisdom of calling Milledufleur.

"Hello," she said.

"Good evening, it's Kim David."

"This is an unexpected pleasure. Are you back in Morocco?"

"No, I had some unfinished business in Holland, so I thought I'd wrap that up before going to Morocco."

"Oh, I see. When will I see you again? We talked about future assignments but nothing specific."

"Actually, that is why I called. There are a number of details I need to review with you."

"When?"

"Very soon."

He rang off and sat there thinking of her. Soon, he knew, it would be soon.

Michael Gilmartin returned to his desk in the St. Louis FBI office after his meeting with his boss Jim Donovan. Gilmartin's brain was on fire. Donovan reviewed and tried to explain the offer that Gilmartin had received from the FBI headquarters. The offer was to be a Legal Attaché in Brussels, Belgium. After graduating from law school ten years ago, Michael had worked in the Chicago office and had transferred to the St. Louis office three years ago.

Donovan was a man of few words, always direct and to the point. His point to Michael was simple: this was one hell of an opportunity, but Washington wanted an answer by morning. Donovan told him it was urgent—he would be replacing Tom Turner, who had been in Brussels for more than five years. Turner had accumulated massive information on Abu Awami in the course of his duties. The Bureau was convinced that Awami's group was responsible for the recent attempted assassination of Shlomo Argov, the Israeli Ambassador to the U.K. This attempt on Argov's life precipitated Israel's invasion of Lebanon.

Gilmartin was elated—the only complication was Judy Brown, the woman he had been seeing for the last four years. Their involvement was intimate. He was sure she would tell him to marry her and take her with him. Problem was he didn't want to make an honest woman of Miss Brown. Physically, they were compatible, but, at least in his mind, they were far apart mentally. He was almost certain what his decision would be. Opportunities like this, if not taken, were not likely to be repeated.

Milledufleur Rose had been in Brussels for a month in her position as "Visiting" Professor on Middle East Studies at the University of Brussels. The assassination of Anwar Sadat was just two months ago. Her rebuff of Drew Cahill coincided with the date of Sadat's assassination.

She was reviewing a quickie exam she had sprung on her class of twenty five—most of the students were Wallons, but five of the students were Flemish. She conducted the class in French to the consternation of the Dutch speakers. This was symbolic of the tension between the two main language sects of Belgium. She was fluent in French and German as well as in Hebrew and Arabic. She went to the apartment's bar and poured herself a large glass of Cabernet. As she settled on her divan, her phone rang—it was Kim David on the line.

"Milly, it's Kim. I'll be over in a flash."

True to his word, within minutes, he entered her apartment at 25 Rue Gerard. He hustled up the stairs, pushed open the door, and enjoyed her passionate embrace and open mouth kiss.

"God, it's good to see you Kim—you are still my charmer. Glass of whiskey?"

"Sure, three fingers. What are you serving these days?"

"Glenlivet—does that meet with your approval?"

"You bloody well know it does."

"I know the number two man of the Mossad has an important assignment for me. I just hope it's not too dangerous."

Kim smiled as he took a swallow of the scotch. He explained that this was a critically important job the Mossad wanted her to do. He opened his briefcase and took out a folder labeled "Allawi al Otaibi, aka Abu Awami."

"Merde," she cried.

"Don't fret—you will have expert help."

"Who?"

He pushed another folder to her, this one labeled "Michael Gilmartin."

She opened the folder and went through the contents that revealed the background of Michael Gilmartin. He was a graduate of St. Louis University's School of Law. He joined the FBI after his graduation in 1975 and was assigned to the FBI's Chicago office. He worked out of Chicago until 1982, when he was transferred to St.

Louis, his hometown. There were several photos of Gilmartin, which she thought revealed a rather handsome young man with black hair and an engaging smile. Milly liked what she saw, at least physically. She wondered what he would be like in person. Well, she thought, we will find out shortly.

She smiled at Kim before asking him, "When will I meet this Michael Gilmartin?"

"I can read that smile," said Kim. "He has the looks that you like—I'm sure that you will find him to your liking. He could become one of your many conquests— seems that you have developed a, shall we say, an affinity to American men."

"Kim, you know I enjoy sexual affairs, but now, you are referring to my assignment to seduce Drew Cahill, the oil man. Believe me, that was an assignment from you and the Mossad—it was just a job."

"A job you did with aplomb; however, I know you had some delicious moments with Mr. Cahill. It wasn't 'all work and no play.'"

"Kim, you are my strongest sexual attraction."

"Strongest, but not only," smiled Kim.

CHAPTER 2

Ghanem al Ghanem, a true Saudi Arabian, had a problem. The Request for Quotation (RFQ) just released by Getty could be a bonanza for Ghanem— problem was he didn't know anyone who had the expertise to do what the RFQ requested. None of his so-called Palestinian experts had any experience operating an "integrated" tug & barge operation to deliver crude oil to the small refiners of Iraq, Iran, Syria, Jordan, and Qatar.

Ghanem fully understood the potential the RFQ presented. Getty had "in-house" markets for 75,000 barrels/day (b/d) of crude to be split between its refinery in Delaware and its joint venture with Mitsubishi in Tokyo. These two refineries were designed to refine the high sulphur content crude that Getty had produced from his Saudi concession located in Kuwait. No other refinery in the world was designed to process the dirty crude except the small refineries in Iraq, Syria, Jordan, and Qatar. The quality standards of these smaller refineries were so low that they could refine "sludge" and sell it in these desperate markets. The potential was nearly $20 million per annum.

This was some five times the amount of income Ghanem generated from his current contracting with Getty and the tomato farms in southern Kuwait. Ghanem had plenty of money from his royal family contacts in his native city of Hail, Saudi Arabia (his uncle was Olliman Sulyman). In Ghanem's mind, there was never enough money. Neither Saudi nor Kuwait was politically stable. Deposits in Beirut, London, and New York were a hell of a lot more stable in Ghanem's mind.

Ghanem sat back at his Wafra farm and sipped his smuggled $100/bottle of Johnny Walker Red. He knew Ted Collins, Getty's Manager of Engineering and Contracts, had received his note asking Ted to meet him at his farm. Ted and the Saudi contractors scratched each other's backs, profitably.

Predictably, Ted's pickup pulled up to Ghanem's shack within the hour. Ted ambled up to Ghanem's shack and knocked. Ghanem welcomed Ted warmly. "Ahlan wa Sahlan," uttered Ghanem, and he embraced him in the Arab manner.

Ghanem slowly explained his problem to Ted. Ted smiled, "I know who can solve your problem. He did work for Getty and others in Delaware, Southern California, and the UK. He is good and reliable and won't rob you blind. Here is his business card."

The card displayed the name "Michael Burdick, Barge Operations, New York, and Vancouver."

"Do you want me to call him? I can explain the set-up and what Getty wants. Basically it's pretty straight forward. Basically all the production over 75,000 b/d is put back, losing about 2800 to 3000 b/d. This could produce a pure profit of $10 million per annum, even after capital and operating costs."

Ghanem clucked with his tongue as Saudis do when they get excited. This money would buy him more Lebanese whores that he could use, with plenty of money left over.

"Please call him, Ted."

"You understand he isn't going to make the trip from New York to Kuwait on his own dime. Also, he will want a consulting fee—he's not cheap."

Ghanem wasn't deterred in the least. "When can he come?"

"Ghanem, I will call him and send a copy of the RFQ to him, but I don't know if he can or will come. He's busy with a project, and I also hear he has a new involvement with a beautiful widow."

"He wouldn't need to be here long, maybe a week. Of course, he can't bring his woman here."

"Understood, I'll call him tomorrow."

"Ted, you know I'll make a deposit in your Swiss bank account."

Ted smiled and shook Ghanem's hand.

By using Getty's long distant operator in Los Angeles, Ted finally was connected to Mike Burdick the following morning. As ridiculous as it may seem, international connections, while a bother, were at least possible compared to local calls within Kuwait. Ted and Mike knew each other fairly well from Burdick's involvement in Getty's operations in California and Delaware. Ted summarized the situation to Burdick who, surprisingly to Ted, expressed interest in the project.

"When can you come to Kuwait?" he asked Burdick.

"Get the RFQ to me as soon as possible—I'll look at it and let you know. If it's as lucrative as you say, I'll be damn interested."

"I'll send it by Getty courier—it should be there in two days. Mike, this could be fun. You know most of the Getty guys over here and the Saudis are a real piece of work, especially Ghanem."

CHAPTER 3

Milly was looking forward to the evening's small gathering of the "Friends of the University of Brussels." The list of attendees was small but select. Michael Gilmartin, the FBI Legal Attaché to Belgium, was on the list. Kim David had stressed to her that she must secure a close and, he emphasized, very close relationship with Gilmartin.

The Israeli Prime Minister had instructed the Mossad that the neutralization of the Abu Awami Organization was of the highest priority. The attempted assassination of Shlomo Argov, the Israeli Ambassador to the United Kingdom, in 1982 by the Abu Awami Organization was the forcing function. Argov survived the assassination attempt but would remain paralyzed for the rest of his life. The wanton killings, not just of Israelis but also of Palestinians who were cooperative with Israelis, had to be stopped.

Gilmartin's predecessor Tom Turner had built a thorough file on Abu Awami's Organization. It was time for the Mossad, namely Milly, to get Gilmartin to help them eliminate these killers.

The "mixer" was being held at the Conrad on Avenue Louise. The spacious Conrad had a lobby bar area that was reserved for this evening's soirée. It was perfectly suited for the one hundred or so invitees. The grand piano located to the rear of the room was being played by the black man, Harry Green, who was imported from New Orleans for the summer. The soothing touch was a perfect background for this crowd and room.

Milly arrived slightly early—she wanted to be there when her quarry Michael Gilmartin arrived. She had chosen a black cocktail dress that revealed her tempting body. Black gloves framed her arms up to her elbows. The party was scheduled to last an hour and a half. The start of the party was at 7 pm—the timing was scheduled so as to not interfere with the balance of the attendees' evening.

Milly positioned herself near the front of the lobby area. Each of the participants was given an identification tag that indicated his or her name, position, and organization. Milly's simply stated "Milledufleur Rose, Professor, Middle Eastern Studies, University of Brussels." Since she was reasonably new to the Brussels community, she was thankful for the ID tags. She accepted a flute of champagne from one of the fifteen waiters. Each of the attendees was greeted by the President of the University, two lovely young ladies, members of his staff, and the Director of Community Relations, a jovial looking middle-aged man by the name of Pierre Gustin.

She anxiously observed the arrival of the evening's guests. Since the mixer was a Brussels University function, she played her role and greeted each attendee. There were several NATO representatives and members of the European Community replete with wives, mistresses, or husbands, as the case might be. After about a half hour passed, she became a little nervous—no Michael Gilmartin yet. She knew that he did respond positively to the RSVP.

She mixed well and had brief, smiling greetings with most of the arrivals, and then, at 7:20, her target arrived.

They had never met; she was a bit unsettled, as she first had the thought that he might ignore her. She quickly dismissed the thought, as that had never happened before. She always got her man. She watched him come up the steps to the lobby bar and quickly approached him as he completed the greeting by the University President and his welcoming group.

"Michael Gilmartin, welcome to the mixer. I am Milly Rose, also a newcomer to Brussels. I did have a chance to meet your predecessor Tom Turner but only briefly after my arrival in Brussels."

Michael smiled at Milly and returned the greeting. "Tom is an interesting guy and was doing some important work here, but it was time to move on. Almost five years is a long posting for us."

"Michael, I don't want to monopolize your time. I know you want to meet others, but don't stray too far, as I do want to talk to you." She grabbed his arm for emphasis and gently but firmly rubbed her leg against his. She smiled broadly as she mouthed, "Tout a l'heure."

As Milly maneuvered through the crowd, she chatted mostly with the men hosting IDs that displayed "European Community" or "NATO"—a largely unimpressive and unexciting group, in her mind. She was watching Gilmartin, and the more she saw of him, the more she liked what she saw. She decided it was time to make her move.

Michael was near the rear of the room, close to the piano and to Harry Green, who was producing a nice bit of background music. He was engaged by two couples who were not of his age. They seemed pleasant and relaxed by the vin blanc they were freely imbibing. She very deftly moved into a position where she was alongside Gilmartin. She told the couples that she hoped they had enjoyed the party but that she had to have a word with Michael before she had to go. They acknowledged her and thanked her for the evening as she took his arm and steered him toward the front of the lobby.

"Sorry to be so forward, but I do want to talk to you. This party will be breaking up soon. Might I suggest that we have a talk somewhere other than here? I'll be saying my goodbyes and be out of here in five minutes. Down Avenue Louise, not more than one hundred meters to the right, is a bar/restaurant called Rick's Place, a take-off of Rick's Place in the movie Casablanca. It's a bit potty but a good place to talk. I'll be there and take a table, please don't disappoint me, say in ten minutes. Besides, it's close to the Conrad, your interim home." She gave him a smile, maintained eye contact, and kissed his cheek as she sauntered away.

He watched her as she moved toward the exit. He smiled to himself. What a gorgeous woman, he thought. He couldn't believe what he thought was his good fortune. Rick's Place it is, he thought. He wondered what her game was, but he would find out and soon.

CHAPTER 4

Mike Burdick, according to his peers, was a brilliant naval architect, mathematician, and financial analyst who could do complicated discounted cash flows in his head.

What Burdick couldn't do was have meaningful relationships with women. His last experience was a disaster, lasting long enough to bring him to the pinnacle of bliss and then into the abyss of disaster and remonstration.

This last attempt persuaded him to abandon any attempt for a meaningful relationship. He would confine himself to one-night stands when the need or urge struck. He found the use of prostitutes to be most efficient—no wasted time.

After his father died, Burdick, as the now sole owner of Burrard Shipyards in Vancouver, sold the business for $65 million after taxes. The closing was set for two years hence. He would receive half the funds now and the other half three years hence. His lawyers and financial analysts assured him there would be no problems with the elongated close.

He would have the money needed to pursue his dream ambition—the design and construction of the sailboat that would win the prestigious "America Cup."

His plan was to move to New York where he would do the design and the construction of "America Molera," the sailboat that would win the "America Cup." Burdick bought a town house in the city, where he would design and supervise the construction of the sailboat that would win the "America Cup," but he would summer in Peconic, Long Island. This location would afford him the opportunity to sail, an activity that he enjoyed and that allowed him the time to relax and recharge his batteries. Sailing he could control, a relationship with a woman he couldn't control. Sailing also gave him the chance to entertain the people he needed to raise the rest of the money to help finance the boat's construction.

Nearly two years had gone by since he made his move to New York. Weather permitting, he would sail every day he spent in Peconic, Long Island.

He first noticed her on his initial sail on Peconic Bay. She walked the beach looking out to sea as if she were searching for something or someone. She spent each morning walking and looking out to sea in what he sensed was a ritual of some sort. A ritual of what, he wondered. She began the first of June and, by the beginning of September, disappeared. He would find out why during his nightly visits to the taverns in Peconic Bay, Long Island.

He noticed her immediately as he sailed in the bay. She wore a captain's jacket and a blue felt cap. She wore light blue kulats, which revealed well-shaped and attractive legs and torso. As his curiosity grew, he would sail closer to get a better view of her countenance. She was more than just attractive, he thought—she was beautiful. She looked to be somewhere between thirty-five and forty. She was definitely in his age category and surely appealing.

What could this ritual be, he wondered. Why this almost religious procession? What was it? He couldn't guess, but later, as he talked to the locals over drinks at the taverns, it was revealed.

On one of his sails into the bay, he had James Andrews, a potential investor from New York, on board. "James, do you see that woman walking on the shore looking out to sea?"

15

"I'm not blind Mike. Sure I noticed her—she is a doll."

"Do you know her?"

"No, but I wish I did."

It was a balmy night in late September as Mike was talking to some of the patrons of the tavern over drinks. He related his tale of this attractive woman walking on the beach and looking out to sea as if searching or waiting for someone to sail in.

John Dolan, one of the regulars and a local, told Burdick that the woman he was describing was Jenny Moran. She taught high school at St. Mary's. That explained her disappearance at the beginning of September and her re-emergence at the beginning of June.

"John, you seem to know her. What is what I call a ritual all about?" asked Mike.

Dolan told Burdick that Jenny Moran was married to Dan Moran, who was a captain of a fishing vessel until six years ago, when he and his crew perished during a huge Nor'easter that sank their boat.

"That, my friend, is the story behind the ritual, as you call it. None of us know if she still hopes he will return or if it's in his honor."

Burdick started his second season of sailing. He was pleased with the progress he had made in the design, the financing, and the start of construction at a local shipyard. This was his métier.

He sailed closer to the shore, and there she was, dressed in the same manner, walking and looking out to sea, expectantly, he thought.

He didn't know what possessed him or how he managed to overcome his fear, but he did. He beached the sailboat and approached her.

"Jenny, pardon my effrontery, but my name is Mike Burdick. I've observed you walking on the beach in what appeared to be almost a ritual. I've learned from some of the men on Long Island that you are the widow of a sea captain who perished in a horrific storm six years ago."

He continued, "I just wanted to meet you. I'm single and unattached. Maybe we could have dinner and chat."

She gave him a smile and gently patted his arm. "Mike Burdick, what took you so long? Let's have dinner, and you can tell me about your 'America Cup' project."

CHAPTER 5

Gilmartin checked his watch as he watched Milly gingerly take the steps down from the lobby bar and gracefully take the stairs down and out the main entrance of the hotel. He knew he had time to take the lobby elevator to his room on the fifth floor, number 523. The lobby was full of people—some from the University's party, some going to one of the bars and dining rooms of the Conrad for an evening of entertainment and dining. Michael was impressed with the Conrad— the rooms were large and well-furnished, but the pieces de resistance were the bars and restaurants. One could find entertainment, dining, and companionship within the hotel. He wasn't looking forward to moving into the flat the FBI had rented for him on Rue des Pierres.

He exited the elevator and headed with some urgency to his room. As he entered the room, the room's phone was ringing. He mechanically picked up the phone. "Hello," he uttered.

"Michael, it's Milly. I am at Rick's Place and have a table for two near the entrance. Please hurry, as the flies are buzzing."

"I'll be there in ten minutes or less—I just wanted to freshen up a bit. Save a place for me," he chuckled.

He changed his coat and tie, quickly shaved, and splashed on some aftershave. He hurried out of the room and began his walk down Avenue Louise to Rick's Place and Milledufleur Rose. It was a pleasant spring night, with the sky a pleasant greenish hue. Michael walked at a quick pace—he was anxious, as he wanted to get on with this adventure. He was no stranger to flirtations and the dating scene, but this was not the usual pattern. He was intrigued. Could this have something to do with Tom Turner, his predecessor, he wondered. He also wondered how she knew he had returned to his room—maybe, he thought, it was just a lucky guess.

Michael had not visited Rick's Place. He'd only been in Brussels a few weeks— most of that time he had spent with Tom Turner before Tom returned to the United States. Tom briefed Michael on the file he had built on the Abu Awami Organization. The Awami group wasn't the only Palestinian terror group, but it was, in the eyes of the Belgium government, the European Community, and NATO, the most prolific. At this time, it had mounted terrorist operations in over twenty countries—killing about three hundred people and wounding hundreds more. The Awami Organization was viewed by the intelligence community as the most dangerous terrorist organization.

Michael arrived at Rick's Place within the ten minutes he had told Milly he would take. He could see from the sidewalk that behind the exterior glass casing, which had larger than life size photos of Bogart as Rick and Ingrid Bergman as Ilsa from the Casablanca movie, was a cavernous joint that housed Rick's Place. He opened the door and was promptly greeted by a giant of a maître d'. He guessed the owners of Rick's wanted to stop trouble before it began. The joint was smoke-filled and noisy as the band located on the bandstand played jazz of the time. An attractive woman in a light cocktail dress that left nothing to the imagination began to sing "As Time Goes By" to the accompaniment of a spinet piano played by a Sam look-a-like.

He guessed there were about one hundred tables in addition to a bar that ran some two hundred feet on the far side of the joint. It seemed to him that the place was more than half-filled. It took him a minute or so before his eyes became accustomed to the light and the smoke. There she was at a table for two not more than fifty feet from the entrance. She stood and gestured for him to join her. My God, he thought, what a gorgeous piece of work she is—I'll be lucky not to swallow my tongue, he mused.

They embraced each other in the French manner. He didn't know what her perfume was, but it was intoxicating, just as she was. She sat and pushed her chair as close to his as possible. This should be more than interesting—it will be exciting, he thought. He also thought he could skip dinner and have her for dessert instead.

She held his eyes steady as if she might look inside and find some understanding of who he was. Truth is that she knew more about him than he did of her. That would soon change.

"Michael, thanks for meeting me. I want to get to know you, and I have some matters I want to share with you. But first things first, I don't know if you are satisfied with the food served at the mixer or if you would like to have something else to eat. I must confess that this is not fine dining—the food is tres ordinaire. You do speak French?"

"Yes, I can hold my own in French, even though I lived all my life till now in St. Louis and Chicago. My mother insisted I learn French as a small boy. While French may not still be the language of diplomats, it has served me well, especially here in Brussels. Unless you are famished, why don't we skip dinner and have a drink instead?"

"I think your mother was wise. French is still a useful language to know—it can serve you well in many parts of the world. I would like that drink—a Chevalier-Montrachet, s'il vous plait."

Gilmartin signaled to the hovering waiter, who responded with a too large smile and a well-rehearsed bow. "What is your pleasure, Monsieur?"

"The lady will have a glass of Chevalier-Montrachet, and I'll take a Jameson, over ice." The waiter bowed, repeated the order, and scurried away to secure their libations.

The dance floor was filling with patrons of Rick's, generally older men in business suits accompanied by younger women with tight-fitting and revealing gowns. Michael smiled to himself as he thought, Rick's is a real body swamp.

"Michael Gilmartin, I can read your mind. The smirk gives you away."

He smiled and shook his head. Their waiter approached with the drinks. They sat and eyed each other before Milly proposed a toast. "Here is to a long and mutually agreeable relationship."

Michael wondered what the fuck that meant. "Care to dance?" he asked.

She smiled and stood. "Avec plaisir."

She rose and took his arm in hers and slowly wended her way to the dance floor with him in tow.

CHAPTER 6

Burdick was understandably pissed. He was replaying the meeting he had had with Bill McCormick, Senior Partner at Usher, Riley & Morrish, the law firm handling the sale of Burdick's Burrard Shipyards. URM, as Burdick referred to the firm, had offices in New York, Toronto, Vancouver, and Seattle. The firm had represented Burrard Shipyards for as long as Mike could remember.

McCormick had called Mike and requested an urgent meeting at Burdick's New York City office. When Burdick questioned him what the urgency was all about, McCormick said there were some issues about the closing. Burdick screamed, "What issues?! You bastards told me that there were no issues and that, while the closing was a couple of years in the future, there would be no problems!"

McCormick showed up at Burdick's city office with two junior partners. McCormick explained that half of the closing could be delayed, as a British Columbia Indian tribe was suing Burrard, claiming it had title to the land the shipyard sat on.

Mike realized that his cash windfall was cut in half potentially, and, even if he eventually prevailed, he had a case of the "shorts." He needed some money quick, or his dream of the "America Cup" was in danger. He had no choice—he had to follow up on the opportunity that Ted Collins, Getty Oil's Engineering and Contracts Manager in Kuwait, presented. The content of the RFQ would be a piece of cake for him, but he had to go to Kuwait and do a deal with the

Saudi contractor Ghanem al Ghanem. He wasn't anxious to break the news to Jenny Moran.

He thought he had better move quickly. He needed to talk to Ted Collins and get the arrangements for a visit to Kuwait and to see the Saudi Ghanem al Ghanem. If only Getty Kuwait had a fax machine, the communication would be much easier. Mike was somewhat familiar with the Getty Kuwait operation through his Getty Los Angeles contacts. From what he had picked up from Bill Williams, VP of International Operations, and his technical staff, Kuwait was a Getty operation that was stuck in the 1950s from a communications standpoint. Kuwait was Getty's only international operation—Getty's other operations outside of the U.S. were all "farm-ins" where Getty had minority interest and no control over the operation.

Mike caught up with Ted Collins and made the arrangements for him to go to Kuwait. Ghanem would be the legal sponsor for Burdick. Ghanem would send a first class round trip ticket—KLM New York to Zurich, Zurich to Kuwait City via Swiss Air. Ghanem would have Hassan Salam, a Palestinian employee, to get Burdick through immigration and customs and to his hotel in Fahaheel (an SAS). Collins told Burdick he could, as a Christian non-Muslim, bring in two bottles of alcohol. The sale of alcohol was not allowed in Kuwait. Alcohol was available only on the black market. Ghanem had a black market pipeline—expensive but plentiful.

Getty's offices were located in Mina Saud some thirty miles south of Fahaheel and nearly fifty miles south of Kuwait City. Mina Saud was also the deep water port where the oil was transshipped to Delaware and Japan. The tug and barge operation Burdick would put together would ship out of Mina Saud. Getty had recently built a new jetty, which would be ideal for the tug and barge operations. Mina Saud was also the camp where some thirty American, British, and Palestinian families lived and worked and were surrounded on three sides by 5,000 Saudis. No one knew how many dependents lived there, and, in Wafra, each Muslim man could have up to four wives with any number of offspring. In spite of the numbers, the Americans ran the operation. Burdick knew the top three Americans from the Getty Los Angeles and London offices. J. Paul Getty lived in Sutton Place, a very upscale palace outside of London, until his death in 1976.

Collins told Burdick he would leave New York on April 15 and arrive on April 17, allowing for an overnight in Zurich. Burdick knew that the American control over the mass of people was only possible by the cooperation with PETMIN (the Saudi Petroleum Ministry). Most of the Saudis came from or had roots in the eastern side of Saudi Arabia. Many were Shiites in the largely Sunni Saudi Arabia.

The Sunnis were not totally comfortable with the Shiites. The Sunnis had a strong CID (Central Intelligence Division) contingent in the Partitioned Neutral Zone (PNZ) as a precaution. Burdick would spend several boring but stressful weeks in Kuwait. The PNZ, where Getty operated, was established in 1922 by the Ugair Convention. After the defeat of the Ottoman Empire in WW1, the borders of Kuwait and Saudi Arabia were indefinite. The Bedouins moved between both countries as their flocks of sheep wandered according to the weather. No one cared much about this until the discovery of oil in Kuwait in the Burgan Field in 1938. Then the oil people realized that this could mean oil in the PNZ. The mineral rights in the PNZ were divided fifty percent between Kuwait and Saudi Arabia. Recognizing the opportunity, J. Paul Getty quickly moved in and personally began negotiations with the Saudi King in Saud. He outmaneuvered the bureaucratic Aramco by negotiating a historic high royalty and a down payment of $9.5 million. This began Getty's Middle East operations. True to his reputation, Getty oversaw an operation that was as skinflint as his much deserved reputation. After Getty's death in 1976, the management loosened up greatly but could not change the geography and the miserable environmental conditions.

Burdick understood the conditions, especially the Saudi presence. He knew Ghanem would present a difficult negotiation, but he also knew they needed him as much as he needed them, at least he had hoped.

Burdick landed in Kuwait City after a relaxing and pleasant flight due largely to the outstanding Swiss Air stews, or Flight Attendants, as they preferred to be called. Whatever they were called, they were great. They had fun teasing him when he told them where he was going. "When do you get out of that hot spot?" asked the Senior Attendant.

"I'm not sure—maybe two or three weeks." He replied. They all laughed. "Enjoy the desert."

As he deplaned, he felt the heat, which nearly floored him and caused him to gasp for air, even the super-heated oxygen. Good God, he thought, it's only April.

As he entered, he was greeted by Ghanem's Palestinian envoy, Hassan Salem, who was brandishing a large sign board with Mike Burdick highlighted with "Welcome" written in large English and Arabic font. Hassan ushered him through Customs and Immigration with only smiles from the Kuwaiti personnel. He was quick to observe that he was receiving deferential treatment as the other passengers were going through what he thought was standard treatment. He wondered how much that had cost—he was just pleased that the baksheesh was applied to him.

Hassan directed the man carrying Burdick's luggage to the latest model Cadillac in the parking area. Speaking in a loud voice in Arabic, Hassan was clearly berating this Indian. Hmm, Burdick mused, a clear hierarchy. Hassan sped out of the airport, heading south on the best roads an oil-rich nation could provide. As they drove, Burdick nestled in the back seat at Hassan's insistence. Hassan peppered Burdick with a hundred questions, which Burdick answered as quickly as he could. Hassan announced that they had arrived at the SAS Hotel. Burdick exited and entered the lobby. He was reasonably impressed, first with the air conditioning but then with the location. Looking through the glass partitioning, he observed a large, well-appointed swimming pool on the shore of the sky blue Arabian Gulf, which the Arabs renamed the Persian Gulf. He was impressed.

After telling Burdick that the meeting would be at Ghanem's Wafra residence, Hassan asked Burdick what time he wanted to be picked up. "The earlier, the better," said Mike.

"6 am would be good."

CHAPTER 7

Michael was roused from his sleep at 6:30 a.m. by the wake-up call he had requested the night before. He ordered a pot of coffee while he had the operator on the line. He took a quick shower. As he was toweling off, the bellboy knocked, announcing the arrival of the coffee he had ordered. This is just another thing I will miss after I move from the Conrad, thought Michael.

He poured himself a cup of the still-steaming coffee and picked up the copy of the International Herald Tribune. He still couldn't concentrate—he was still sleepy from the restless night he had spent thinking of Milly. He couldn't get her out of his mind. Even after the shower, he could smell her. Thinking back about the night before and the dance he had had with her at Rick's Place, he was both elated and frustrated. He was elated because of the dance and frustrated because she had called the night off after the dance. She had told him she would call him tomorrow. "I want to talk to you about the Abu Awami Organization. We can meet late afternoon tomorrow."

Her beauty and body entranced him. She was most certainly the most exotic woman he had ever known. What could her interest be in the Abu Awami Organization, he wondered. He had to see her. When they were dancing, if you could call it dancing, it was more like a body melt. She nibbled at his ear, pressed her breasts into his chest, and pressed her legs against his groin—he responded as one would expect. In the midst of his reveries, his phone rang.

"Hello," he intoned.

"Michael, it's Milly. I want to thank you for meeting me at Rick's. I enjoyed our brief time together, especially our dance. You are exciting to be with."

Michael didn't know what to say, so he didn't say anything.

"If you can, I would like to take you to La Truffe Noir. It is just a fabulous experience, one of the best, if not the best, in Brussels. Reservations are extremely difficult, but I know the maître d' through the University. We have a spot at 7:30. What do you think?"

What do I think—are you kidding, he thought. "I don't have anything pressing, so sure, I'd love to. Should I meet you there? I gather the reservation is in your name."

"Lovely Michael. But don't meet me there—come by my flat. It's close to the Conrad—it's not even a ten minute walk. And my place is very close to La Truffe Noir. My address is 25 Rue Gerard. Come by, say, at 7:15, and I'll give you a quick tour of my place. I have some art I think you'll like."

"I'll be there. I'm really looking forward to it."

Michael was elated and quickly shed his fatigue, but then he thought about her interest in Tom Turner's work on the Abu Awami Organization. Maybe, he thought, it's not me she is interested in. He was still up about meeting her, like a dog on a bone.

Michael dressed and walked to his office. He said hello to his secretary, Madam LaRoche. She was middle-aged, nondescript but efficient, just as the FBI wanted. He asked her for Tom Turner's file on the Abu Awami Organization. He was familiar with the file and had spent many hours with Tom as Tom went through the file with him. One thing for sure was that Brussels, Belgium, the European Community, NATO, and the U.S. would be thankful when Abu Awami and his organization were history. What is Milly's interest in Abu Awami, he pondered.

He spent the day going through the file. Turner had a number of meetings with the Belgium government bureaucrats. They did know that Awami and his group had had several meetings in Brussels recently. Awami was an indiscriminate killer—his group eliminated nearly as many Palestinians who cooperated with the Israelis as Israelis.

He returned several phone calls and answered cables from Washington before turning off the lights and locking up. Madame LaRoche had left some time ago. He walked down the street that connected to Avenue Louise and went to the Conrad to freshen up before his engagement with Milledufleur Rose.

He exited the Conrad and asked the doorman how to get to 25 Rue Gerard. "Just turn right at the next street, walk down a block, and turn left again—that will be Rue Gerard. Then look at the addresses—you can't miss it. It's a beautiful area. Are you meeting with a dolly?" Gilmartin thanked him and deposited several Belgium Francs in the doorman's waiting hand. Christ, he thought, these guys live on tips, and I need them.

He walked briskly down the tree-lined Rue Gerard. It was a beautiful area—the street was the home to some magnificent buildings, generally two to five stories in height. It was still early and bright. When he came to 25 Rue Gerard, he stopped and rang the bell.

"Michael, if that's you, the door is open. Come on up. If it's not Michael, I have a loaded pistol in my hand."

Michael laughed and opened the door. There she was, standing at the top of a flight of stairs. He looked up at her. She was dressed in a black cocktail dress, and the sunlight was behind her. He swore that she had nothing on under the gown. He quickly climbed the stairs. She greeted him with an open mouth kiss and squeezed him tightly. She took his hands and deftly moved them to all parts of her body. Abruptly, she broke off the contact.

"Come, my dear man, let me give you a quick tour while we are still in the mood— any longer, we might be tempted to stay here. Let's get out of here." Michael took in the immediate area and said, "This is really nice, Milly—so warm and comfortable. I like your paintings and your furnishings."

"Thank you—I adore it. I was fortunate that the University set this up for me. Come, I'll give you the cook's tour. This, as you can see, is the sitting or living area."

She ushered him through the formal dining room, the guest bed and bath, the spacious kitchen, and the piece de resistance, her bedroom.

"This is my favorite room. I enjoy it so much. The dressing area, the sitting area, and the best is that lovely large tub. Great for soaking, reading, and just relaxing."

He looked around the room and took in the paintings that were an eclectic but pleasant mix. He was particularly impressed with the bed—king-sized, to be sure, with a canopy supported by four mahogany spindles. The bedspread was a French country yellow, capped with an assemblage of light blue pillows. The bed stood on a light beige Berber carpet. Silk Persian carpets, containing scenes highlighted by dark blues and deep reds, were strewn in patterned positions around the room.

"The best part of the room for me, at least, is the bed," said Michael. "Everything else to me is in support of that, as a center piece. It is all somewhat baroque, warm but powerful, almost masculine in strength but with soft edges."

She stood with her hands on her hips gazing at him. "From international FBI agent to some kind of swishy interior decorator!

That's versatility for you. Let's get off the bed, figuratively that is, and on to a different activity," she said.

"I wasn't thinking of the bed as an activity center," he smiled.

She smiled at him. "Sure you were, but we don't have the time—our reservation awaits us. My university would not be pleased with me if we were a no-show. Besides, we'll have time for that later."

He let out a low moan at that. "Is that a promise, or are you just forcing me out?"

"I'm not forcing you in. Come, we should leave while you can still walk."

"You have a point," he muttered.

They made their way down the stairs and exited her flat. She took the time to lock the door. "You see, I don't leave the door open for everyone—just handsome young Americans."

"And you are also picking up the tab. It doesn't get any better than this. Well, it could get better."

Milly was impressed with the Breton style edifice of La Truffe Noir. She wasn't sure if it was seventeenth or eighteenth century. It was a two-story building with a copper-clad roof. Paneled lead windows dominated the street level, while French windows opening to the street sat above. Ironically, she had walked by the building many times. It was only three blocks from her apartment. The restaurant was on the corner of Rue Becker and Avenue Nouvelles.

The interior of the first level was simple but impressive. The paneled windows were framed with plain white muslin curtains, tied back. The floor was oak plank with an occasional Persian carpet here and there. The premier etage was divided into three nearly equal-sized rooms. Each room opened to the other, and each room had six tables—a mix of circular and rectangular. The walls were papered with scenes from the seventeenth century countryside on a pink and black background. Most of the first-floor occupants had female companions who were not their wives. A mixture of French, Flemish, English, and Germanic languages was combined into a low murmur that proved inaudible over the violin and cello strains of the chamber music.

No sooner than they had been greeted by the maître d' than a gentleman approached them. It was Alex Bianchi, the proprietor of La Truffe Noir. He warmly welcomed the couple to his establishment. He took Milly's hand, raised it to his lips, and then shook Michael's hand. "Welcome to my place. Your university called me, Madame Rose, and informed me that you and Mr. Gilmartin would be joining us tonight—as a matter of fact, they made the reservation."

"Please follow me. I have reserved a table upstairs tonight that I think you will enjoy. I would also be happy to suggest your courses for tonight, if you would like," said Alex.

Milly smiled warmly at Alex—she could feel the electricity this handsome man generated. Milly smiled at Michael and said, "We'd like that." Alex ushered them up the curved staircase to the room above. The décor was the same as below, except it was divided into alcoves, with tables for two, four, and eight. Alex escorted them to an alcove for two. The table was adorned with a starched white tablecloth, set off with black napkins and black orchids in crystal vases.

"Could I offer you an aperitif?" Alex inquired.

Michael looked at Milly, shrugged, and said, "Sure, a Bombay gin with tonic for the lady, and I'll have a Jameson on the rocks." The attentive waiter standing at Alex's side sprung into action.

Alex nodded as the waiter came back almost instantly with the drinks. "I know you will agree with me that my wares are simply the best in all of Brussels. I would strongly suggest that you start with the carpaccio of tuna, flavored with ginger and just a hint of wasabi. Then, I would say you should take the fresh Breton sea scallops on a potato pancake with le truffe, St. Jean d'été cream, and shavings on top of the scallops. Of course, the tuna will be accompanied by truffles, but only truffles that are in season."

Milly took a deep breath and exhaled. The pungent aroma of the truffles permeated the room. "What do you mean that only truffles that are in season will be served? How many types of truffles are there?" she asked.

Alex was thrilled to expound on his knowledge of the world of truffles, which, of course, was the source of funds he used to underwrite his other two passions in life—golf and women. He couldn't get enough of either. "My dear people, there are ten varieties of the tuber. Most people know only the very expensive black truffle—the melanosporum, which is in season from mid-November through March. The really expensive white Alba truffle is harvested only in October through early December," said Alex. "The truffles you will experience tonight are now in season. The St. Jean d'été is the most plentiful and, I must admit, the cheapest. It is more gray than black but still very tasty. Our belief is that any truffle in season is far superior to a truffle not in season or, perish the thought, to a truffle that is not fresh. We are the best, because we only serve the freshest."

"So," said Michael, "if we were going to have a gray truffle, why do you call your place the 'Black Truffle'? Why not call it the 'White, Black, and Gray Truffle'?"

"You aren't in the sales business—I am. I sell my product for $200 an ounce. It's called bait and switch. Everyone has heard of the black truffle, so, when in season, it is fine. Then we give them the alternative of the very dear Alba truffle. But when not in season, we give them the best truffles available. This also gives us the chance to tell the whole truffle story. People love being snobs and parties to what only a privileged few know. And the best part is they become hooked and are only too willing to pay our ridiculous prices. But, Michael, you know the story. We stimulate their appetites, and then, as the laws of economics dictate, we charge what the truffle traffic will bear," Alex said smiling.

Milly was amused by Alex's passionate lecture about a fungus that grows underground and is rooted out by pigs. She was sure he was a shrewd businessman. She was also sure that he was a very attractive man, about as tall as Michael, with also an athletic build that nicely filled out his expensive Briony suit. He wore his light brown hair full and combed straight back. His full mustache nicely framed a delicate mouth that set off his white teeth. He had a dazzling smile, but she noticed that his hazel eyes were flat. They didn't twinkle like Michael's did when he smiled. Milly said, "Well, thanks. The aroma here is nice, almost sensual. Do you find that these truffles have an aphrodisiac effect?"

"I will only suggest that, after your experience here, you let me know," said Alex.

Milly said, "But of course."

What did that mean, thought Michael. Everything she said and every motion she made unleashed a torrent of sensations. He was determined to be cool and reserved, although he knew she was going to tease him into making a move that she would probably rebuff. He was resolute that he wouldn't take the bait and put her in control. Besides, she wants something he has. He said to Alex, "How about your wine recommendations?"

Alex winked at Milly before turning to address Michael. "I would recommend a bottle of Puligny-Montrachet, premier cru, 'Clos de la Pucelle. And, to seal the deal, the wine will be with my compliments."

Milly squeezed Michael's arm where her hand was resting and smiled at Alex. "You are as generous as you are charming, Monsieur."

"Thank you, both of you. It's been a pleasure. Enjoy this dining experience, as I'm sure you will," said Alex. He handed both of them his business card and asked them for both for theirs. "You never know when we may be in contact. And, as I said, please let me know your impressions of your experience with tonight's dining experience."

Milly said, "Alex, thank you, and you will certainly hear from me."

Michael thought this was a pretty overt move on her part, but he also thought for whatever reason she or the University was picking up the tab. There had to be a good reason. He didn't think it was because of his super personality.

Milly raised her glass to Michael for a toast. "A votre santé," she uttered. He replied, "A votre." They sipped their drinks and echoed a "tres bien." Dinner arrived, and they slowly devoured the tuna carpaccio, both emitting low moans of pleasure. An exchange of glances and silent expressions said it all. It was divine.

They exited the restaurant, and she invited him to her flat for a nightcap. "I still have questions about the Abu Awami Organization." They talked about the dinner as they walked the short distance to her flat. They arrived, and she unlocked the door and led him up the stairwell. Michael was having some second thoughts about his encounter with Milly Rose. As a professor of Middle East Studies at the University of Brussels, what academic interest could she have in the Abu Awami Organization, he wondered. He doubted she would be covering the organization in her lectures, other than going into the history of the various Palestinian terror groups and their impact on the ongoing turmoil in Israel and indeed on the Palestinian peoples. He knew what his interest in her was—it certainly wasn't academic. She was the most attractive, seductive woman he had ever encountered. Reality was most probably that she wasn't attracted to him, but he had something she needed. The question is, what? He was also sure that she would jump Alex Bianchi's bones in a New York minute. So what, he thought, why not enjoy the ride? He wasn't about to divulge state secrets to an enemy agent.

She bade him to have a seat and then brought him a drink—Jameson on the rocks. She poured herself a glass of Chardonnay and settled next to him on the settee. They clinked their glasses in a toast.

"You know I enjoy being with you, but what interest does a college professor have in a terrorist organization like the Abu Awami Organization? Are you what you say you are, or are you a front for another entity?"

"I'll try to explain, but, in the meantime, excuse me while I get into something more comfortable. I shan't be long."

She returned in a sheer black night gown that didn't conceal anything. He could only moan as she took his hand and led him to the bed. "You were impressed with my bed earlier—now I'll show you how to use it." She shed the gown and led him into her. He could only say, "Oh my God."

CHAPTER 8

Mike Burdick was up, dressed, and ready to go by 5:45a.m. Ted and Hassan both told him that the dress was "casual." He interpreted that to mean khakis and a short-sleeved sport shirt. He picked up a coffee from the hotel restaurant and walked to the lobby. Hassan pulled up promptly at 6 a.m. Burdick, lugging a large black brief case, got into the waiting car. Christ, he said to himself, it's already boiling.

He didn't bother to greet Hassan in his pigeon Arabic, since Hassan was fluent in English. "Good morning, Mr. Burdick. I see you have a coffee from the hotel. I also have a thermos for you that holds four cups of hot coffee. It is a long ride to Wafra. If you need to stop to relieve yourself, just let me know. This is just the barren desert, so we won't see hardly anyone after we are past Mina Saud."

"Thanks, Hassan. Ted Collins will be there, right?"

"Oh, yes, he will go directly to Ghanem's Wafra office." Wafra was the last of Getty's gathering stations in which crude oil was put into a pipeline and was transported to Getty's storage tanks at Mina Saud. At Mina Saud, the crude oil was then piped out to the crude carriers that called on the port twice a month. Wafra was one of the Getty main oil fields and home to many of the Saudi workers. It was also Ghanem's home. Ghanem lived in Wafra, where he also had a large farm that sat on top of a desert well, which provided Ghanem all the water needed to irrigate his farm. Ghanem grew tomatoes and dates from his palm trees, and he extracted oil from the palm trees. Ghanem considered himself a true farmer as well as one of the ten Saudi contractors who did all of the Getty contract work. The Saudi contractors proved to be, with the Palestinians who managed all the Getty contracts, as efficient, if not more efficient, than Aramco, which was located further south in the Saudi Arabian desert. Aramco was run by the employees of the Seven Sisters, which were comprised of all American oil companies with the exception of British Petroleum. The work then was done largely by the American employees who were well paid and who received substantial fringe benefits. Given their monopolistic position in the market place, the cost of production was not a consideration. Getty, with its much lower cost of production, did it the Getty way. A handful of Americans' and Brits' pay packages and fringe benefits were dwarfed by the Aramco payouts. Compared to the Seven Sisters, Getty was like the bastard cousin. Aramco also had the most prodigious reserves in the world and produced a sweet (low sulphur) crude that was in demand worldwide. Getty produced 75,000 b/d of sour crude, while Aramco produced one hundred times that with crude that literally oozed out of the ground—nearly a zero cost of extraction. Getty, not surprisingly, was a lot like Ghanem. It wasn't pretty, but it worked for them.

As Hassan sped down the paved highway, Burdick couldn't help but observe that the sand was indeed dirty, not the magnificent dunes depicted in Saudi Arabian public relations documents. "Christ, Hassan, this is filthy— how can a desert be filthy?"

Hassan laughed, "This is the Partitioned Neutral Zone of Kuwait. Just wait—it will get worse. Wait till you see Wafra and the Wafra desert."

"Ghanem has money. He could live in a nicer place, say Kuwait City or even Salamiah. Why does he live in Wafra?"

"Because he is a true Saudi Arabian—this is all that he knows or wants to know. He loves the desert. He is the Sheik of Wafra, and he is admired by his people. The only times he has been outside of this area are on occasional trips to Beirut to lie with the Lebanese whores."

Well, he thought, this is no trip to Hollywood, but, according to Ted Collins, once Ghanem gives you his word, he sticks to it. It's the honor of the desert, according to Collins.

"Hassan, are Bill Arthur, George Padgett, and Jim Morris in Mina Saud now?" asked Burdick.

"Oh, yes, and also Gino Perretti—they are all so anxious to see you."

"It's been a while, but I've known those guys for a while—good people. I did some work in the States and Canada for them."

Why in the world didn't we just have the meetings in Mina Saud, he wondered

"Hassan, why didn't we just have the meeting in Mina Saud—do you know?"

"Oh, I don't know exactly, but I think Ghanem has some people he wants you to meet," said Hassan.

Burdick was at a loss. They would have to go to Mina Saud in any case. Wafra wasn't in the picture—it wasn't a port. By now, they were travelling on hard- packed sand roads, for, as far as one could see, there was nothing but hard-packed sand, a dirty brown colored sand. Hassan continued driving west. He confided to Burdick that Americans would be lost in five minutes—without a guide, there was no way the Americans could find their way. There were no maps and no landmarks to give the Westerner a clue as to where they were. The westerners who resided in Mina Saud could find a specific destination, such as Ghanem's Wafra office and residence, but to stray from the known path led to the uninitiated confusion and turmoil.

Hassan continued driving in this land of sand—no trees, no landmarks, only the boiling hot sun that brought a haze over the area. Finally, Hassan exclaimed, "We are here!" He pulled up in front of a building of sorts—one-story, rectangular in shape, about three hundred feet in length, its depth not discernible. The construction consisted of sheets of plywood faded irregularly by the sun and the blowing sand. This was the office of the Sheik of Wafra. To the left, separated by about one hundred yards, was the residence that housed Ghanem's family.

Hassan parked the car, and, before they could get out of the vehicle, they were greeted by Ghanem, Ted Collins, and two men who Hassan said were the Palestinian engineers who worked for Ghanem. Ghanem cast an impressive figure—well over six feet tall clad in the white dish dash, replete with the white head dress. Ghanem smiled and welcomed Burdick with a hearty handshake and embrace. He greeted them in Arabic and English. Ghanem's English was broken—heavily accented but understandable.

The Palestinian engineers were dressed in western clothes and greeted Burdick in English. Collins and Burdick greeted each other as long-lost friends, which they almost were. "It's been a while Ted—you don't look any worse for wear. The climate must agree with you," said Burdick.

"Mike, you look great—must be the stay at the SAS Hotel."

"Well, a big difference between here and there. This is, well, a little more primitive," said Mike.

Ted laughed, "'A little more' is an understatement. But wait till you see Mina Saud—a shining city on the beach!"

"Really?" Mike asked.

"Not exactly, but better."

Ghanem's Palestinian engineers were named Elias and Mahmoud. Elias was the older of the two and took charge of the proceedings. He indicated that everyone should go into Ghanem's office and start the meeting. They entered the office where the air conditioners were cranking—not high-tech but effective in keeping the temperature tolerable. The layout was typical Saudi. Seating was on the floor in front of a long table, which was just high enough so that an agile Arab could get his feet under the table. Mike had to, with the aid of pillows, sit and squat in front of the table.

Elias explained that Ghanem had asked that Elias and Mahmound lead the discussion concerning a proposal they could submit to Getty for the transport of crude to ports in Iraq, Iran, Syria, Jordan, and Qatar. Ted told the group that Mike Burdick, as the owner of Burrard Shipyards in Vancouver, had experience in building and operating integrated tug and barge operations in California, Delaware, the U.K., and on the Great Lakes.

Mike took over the meeting. He explained that he had carefully examined the requirements of the Getty RFQ. "Gentlemen, we are in a position to comply with requirements of Getty, and, within eight weeks, we can be sailing to Mina Saud. I have an integrated tug and barge system that just came off hire. It was transporting newsprint from Quebec City to ports in Thunder Bay, Ontario and Duluth/Superior, Minnesota. I would retrofit the barge so it would have a capacity of 10 million barrels a year. I will time-charter this system to Ghanem for $4300/day for five years firm." In addition, Burdick proposed that he receive a rider of $1000/day as his cut of the profits. Burdick told Ghanem and his representative that he would require a bank guarantee to cover the time-charter and the $1000/day cut of profits.

Elias, Ghanem's Palestinian engineer, objected to Burdick's proposal, saying that Burdick was asking too much and taking no risk. Burdick shrugged and, in effect, said, "Take it or leave it." Ghanem knew that this was a good deal and informed the room that he would accept the Burdick proposal. Ghanem and Burdick shook hands. Burdick produced the agreement that his lawyers had prepared.

"Good, we have a contract, Mr. Burdick," said Ghanem. Ghanem stood and shook Burdick's hand. Ted Collins suggested that they go to Mina Saud and present their proposal to Getty—they could get approval almost immediately. Since Collins was Manager of Contracts and Engineering, that seemed to be a done deal. Getty's PNZ General Manager was sure to sign off. Ghanem clapped his hands, and two Indian servants appeared. Ghanem offered all Johnny Walker Red to toast to the deal.

Burdick declined the offer of a drink at that time of day—he had more ground to cover before he could take his eye off the ball. He needed to get to Mina Saud and also make sure the money was in his account in New York. The Palestinians acted as if this were a holiday inspired by their brilliance. Hassan, as a good Lebanese, didn't drink in any case. Burdick took note of this—Hassan could be a useful, reliable connection.

As Hassan, Burdick, and Ted Collins prepared to drive to Mina Saud and conclude the business with Getty, the relative calm of Ghanem's camp was suddenly shattered by the sound of cars and pickups screeching to a halt, followed by shouts in Arabic and the discharge of weapons in the air. The door burst open, and five men, who had rifles strapped around their shoulders and revolvers shoved in their belts, burst into the room. They were led by a short, balding nondescript middle-aged man wearing a black cap that didn't cover his balding head. He surveyed the room—he acknowledged the two Palestinians with a nod, a smirk more than a smile, and greeted

Ghanem in Arabic and in accordance with Arab custom—an embrace and a kiss on both cheeks.

Burdick had no idea what was going on. It was obvious that Ghanem and his Palestinians knew this group—they seemed friendly to each other, but the sudden appearance of armed men did not have a calming effect on Burdick. Hassan sensed Burdick's concern and whispered to him that this was Allawi al Otaibi, better known as Abu Awami, the leading Palestinian terrorist of the time. He told him not to worry—the Abu Awami Organization killed only Jews and Palestinians who were friendly to the Jews. Hassan added that Abu Awami was in Kuwait to raise money for his cause. It was a form of blackmail: pay me and we won't kill you—we will kill the Jew and the Jew sympathizers.

"Hassan, we are finished here. Let's go to Mina Saud. These terrorists scare the crap out of me. I think we should go now," said Burdick.

"Mr. Burdick, don't be nervous. They know better than to touch an American—they know the Americans would kill them all. But you are right—we should go to Mina Saud. We can say good-bye to Ghanem and then go. Ghanem really likes you."

"He has several million reasons to like me," Mike laughed.

CHAPTER 9

MINA SAUD OF THE PNZ

Hassan was silent as he sped east toward the Gulf and the port and Getty facilities that comprised Mina Saud. Burdick asked Hassan how long before they would be at Mina Saud.

"It won't be much longer. We will be at the junction of the Kuwaiti highway and the Kuwaiti road that takes you to Mina Saud—no more hard-packed sand roads."

"Great," said Burdick. Burdick didn't see much change in the scenery as they sped east. What a forlorn place this is, he thought.

"Hassan, these characters this morning, you said they were members of the Abu Awami Organization. They looked pretty dangerous to me, but you said not to worry. Why?"

"Oh, Mr. Burdick, they are dangerous only if you are a Jew or a Palestinian who is friendly to Israel. There aren't many Palestinians who are friendly to the Jew, but there are some. The Saudis and Kuwaitis are smart and rich. They pay money to the Abu Awami Organization as protection so that they won't be bothered by these terrorists. The terrorists spend most of their time in Iraq and Libya. The leader Abu Awami, however, spends much time in rural Poland."

"So, they are in and out?"

"Oh, yes, as I said, they would never harm an American. They know the Americans would chase them down and kill them all."

Burdick shook his head. "Seems like the Israelis would kill them too."

"Yes, but the Israelis took their homeland in Palestine in 1948. The Arabs waged wars against the Jew, which they always lost. But the Palestinian terrorists, especially Abu Awami, will never stop until they are all killed."

What a fucked-up neighborhood this place is, thought Burdick. He was happy he wasn't a Palestinian, terrorist, or ordinary citizen.

Hassan announced that they had now arrived at Mina Saud. Looking east, Burdick saw the sky blue of the Arabian Gulf. To the north was a chain-linked fenced area containing, according to Hassan, the village of Mina Saud where some 5,000 Saudis lived. They were all on the Getty payroll, even though, as Hassan explained, few, if any, did any work. In addition to the goats that roamed free were children of all ages. The older ones wore dish dashes that were once white, while the younger ones, bounding along unencumbered by clothing, shared their space with the desert flies, gnats, and other pestilence. Within the village of Mina Saud, there were three mosques, four elementary schools, and a single-story building that served as the village hospital staffed by Egyptian and Lebanese doctors and nurses.

They then arrived at a gate that guarded the entrance to the Getty oil facilities. These facilities contained storage tanks rising above the desert floor that could hold 125,000 barrels of crude oil and a refinery that could process 20,000 barrels per year. There was also an area fenced-off that housed what was called the Senior Staff Housing and Offices. These offices consisted of eight trailers imported from Getty's Oklahoma trailer manufacturing facility.

To the north was the Senior Staff Housing. Most of the housing consisted of trailers of Getty origin. In addition to the trailers, there were eight adobe-like constructed houses of some substance that bordered on the beautiful Arabian Gulf. These were the residences of the senior staff. American employees lived in all but one of these adobe-constructed houses. The smallest of these houses was reserved for the Chief Medical Officer, who, at that time, was Dr. Sabbagh, an Egyptian doctor. The three other physicians—Palestinian, Lebanese, and Egyptian—were provided with the Getty trailers.

The Egyptian and Lebanese nurses were housed in a segregated area of the village. Even though the nurses were guarded, the resourceful senior staff Saudis found ways to fraternize—a source of friction for the American managers. The Saudi senior staff wives frequently complained to the American managers. In a way, this was comical but, in the minds of the American managers, a royal pain in the ass and a waste of time. In this environment, though, they had plenty of time to waste. Thanks to Ghanem's smuggling and to the managers' purchases outside Kuwait, the American management also had plenty of booze—predominately whiskey and gin. Wine and beer were too bulky to be practical. Some made their own wine from kits smuggled in, but it was of terrible quality. The same was true of "flash," which was distilled from pure grain alcohol. It was a vile and potentially dangerous fluid that only the desperate would drink, but, at times, there were a lot of desperate residents at the camp.

Hassan pulled up to what Burdick found out was the trailer that served at Bill Arthur's office. Mike got out of the car and was immediately greeted by Bill Arthur. It had been a few years, eight to be exact, since he had seen Arthur. Burdick had an integrated tug and barge operation built and delivered for Getty's Ventura, California operation. The operation and the concept for the operation were almost identical to the system that he believed he had sold to Ghanem. He knew he had needed Arthur's blessing, at least for the record. Mike felt this was just a formality. But, as a wise man once said, "It ain't over till it's over."

Arthur and Burdick greeted each other, warmly shaking hands and bearing hugs. "Christ, Bill, what's your secret? You haven't aged a bit."

"You're not bad yourself. As for me, it must be the clean living in the PNZ and Getty camp." They were joined by Padgett, Morris, and Peretti, who all broke into laughter at that remark.

Arthur bade them to follow him to his office. They all took chairs at the long table facing Arthur's desk. TK, Arthur's Indian secretary, brought them all coffee, the favorite drink during the working hours in the PNZ.

"Let's get to the business at hand. Then, we can give Mr. Burdick one of our sumptuous dinners, including the dancing girls," laughed Arthur.

It didn't take long to review Burdick's deal. It was a natural—no one else could have a system ready to go in eight weeks. Ghanem would be taking what little operating risks there were. Bill Arthur indicated that he was happy with the Ghanem/ Burdick deal. He politely asked Padgett, Morris, Peretti, and Ted Collins if they were in agreement. They all indicated that they were.

"Well gents, looks like we have a deal. This will be found money for Getty—I'm surprised we didn't do this a while back."

George Padgett slapped his knee as if for emphasis and said, "Because we didn't have Burdick before!"

They chuckled in unison, and, when Bill Arthur told them the "drinking lamp" was lit, they all mumbled in agreement. They would show Mike Burdick the famous PNZ hospitality. They repaired to Bill Arthur's house. George Padgett led the way. George had a long history in the PNZ—in fact, he was the PNZ's first General Manager. George was a graduate petroleum engineer from Rolla

School of Mines in Rolla, Missouri. After his graduation in 1944, he enlisted in what was then the Army Air Force. He checked out on fighter aircraft, was sent to England, and flew thirteen missions until he was shot down over France. He was captured by the Luftwaffe and escaped. He was then rescued and sheltered by the French underground resistance. He stayed with the French Resistance until Germany surrendered. During this time, he learned to speak in French, with a strong southern Missouri accent. His French would serve him well later in his life.

George had Burdick in tow, and, when they were in front of George's house, George stopped and asked Mike to wait a minute while he picked up his wife, Renée Caspar Padgett. She took Burdick's breath away. She was nearly as tall as George, who was over six feet in height, with a beautiful visage, topped by thick, black hair worn shoulder length. She literally took Burdick's breath away, as she did to all the men who were fortunate enough to meet her.

George was heavily recruited by oil companies when he returned to the States. Getty Los Angeles Human Resources people recognized they had a super candidate on their hands and sent George to London where he would meet and be interviewed by J. Paul Getty. Jean Paul took an immense liking to this Missouri farm boy hero pilot. He instructed his HR people to hire him and send him to their Ventura, California operation for training. When J. Paul began negotiations with the King of Saudi Arabia for the Saudi concession in the PNZ, he knew who would be his General Manager. Klaus von Bulow was J. Paul Getty's all-around enabler. He had style and smarts—besides, he liked the wealthy old lecher.

Burdick had no clue as to what led to Bill Arthur taking Padgett's place as PNZ General Manager. He was intrigued, but, more than that, he was ecstatic to have met Renée Caspar Padgett, as she referred to herself. He figured he would have time to talk to Bill

Arthur tonight. Besides, it didn't change what he was doing. The Getty contract had literally saved his ass.

The entourage wended their way to Bill Arthur's house. When they arrived, they were welcomed by Arthur, Arthur's wife, and a bevy of Arthur's Indian servants. There were at least ten couples in place—a combination of Americans, a few Brits, and the rest Lebanese or Palestinian. The drinks were in ample supply, and, by the din in the room, it sounded as if they were all in good spirits. Burdick did want to talk to the Getty people about what he had experienced this morning with the Abu Awami people. No one seemed disturbed, but he was more than curious.

CHAPTER 10

JACK GALLAGHER

Jack Gallagher thought it was time to call his favorite and only nephew—Michael Gilmartin—to see how he was faring in his new posting as an FBI Legal Attaché in Brussels. After all, he knew it was because of him that Michael joined the FBI after graduating from law school. After retiring as an active FBI agent, Jack joined a Clayton, Missouri law firm, which had a wealthy, if not a bit boring, business practice. Jack had married well—a St. Louis socialite whose family had significant holdings in Monsanto Chemical. Jack didn't have a money problem.

Jack's wife, Lynn Massey, was an only child. Jack and Lynn didn't have any children. This served to enhance Jack's relationship with his nephew. Jack thought of Michael as the son he never had. Jack enjoyed his career as an FBI agent. He had spent most of his FBI career working in Boston. A good part of his efforts were spent pursuing leads about suspected communists. Then-Senator Joe McCarthy (Wisconsin) assembled those suspects through his "Un-American Activity" probes. McCarthy claimed that these suspects posed an internal communist threat against the United States. McCarthy had significant publicity in support of his efforts. Jack enjoyed his work with the FBI, but his new wife was adamant that Jack retire from the FBI and relocate to St. Louis, where Lynn Massey Gallagher's family and money could be put to good use.

Truth was that Jack had almost parental pride in his nephew and would do whatever he could to support his nephew. Michael's assignment as a Legal Attaché was, in Jack's mind, a plum assignment. Jack had always emphasized to Michael that money and position weren't the important things in life. It was the sense of accomplishment—in fact, the thrill and satisfaction of accomplishment—that mattered.

Jack was a competent attorney—systematic and thorough. He was, at forty-five, just ten years or so older than his nephew. He hadn't had much fun in his corporate legal career since he handled a case referred by Mort Bistrisky of Aird & Berlis of Toronto. His client, one Michael Burdick, had a significant contract dispute with a Canadian pulp and paper company. Burdick owned Burrard Shipyards in Vancouver and had a contract with the pulp and paper company, Quebec North Shore Ltd., which was a subsidiary of the Chicago Tribune and New York Post. The suit was about non-performance and was a slam dunk, resolved easily in Burdick's favor. Jack and Mike Burdick became fast friends during this time. They both had a taste for premium vodka, fine wines, and easy women. He and Burdick stayed friends and saw each other periodically in Chicago and in Montreal.

He placed a call to Michael Gilmartin and left a message. An hour later, Michael returned his call. Jack picked up the phone and said, "Michael, it's your favorite uncle. Just called to catch up and see how you are faring in your new assignment."

"Jack, good to hear from you. I'm still getting my feet wet, so to speak. I really like Brussels—it's a great city. The architecture is interesting, the restaurants are super, and living at the Conrad Hotel is excellent. Unfortunately, I'll have to move soon, but it's a nice place and a good location."

"Sounds good. How's the work, or is it too soon to tell?"

"I've met a lot of people—some are very interesting. I have an assignment that is interesting. My predecessor Tom Turner started research on it and has built quite a file. I'm not sure where this will go, but my boss is treating it as top priority. If I ever figure it out, I'll let you know. I don't think I can talk about it yet, or maybe ever."

Jack said, "I understand, but let me know how it's going, when you can. How do you like the women?"

"All I can say is wow! They know how to dress. I did meet a beautiful woman who is a Professor of Middle Eastern Studies. I don't know where this is going, if anywhere. I think it's just an interlude for her. Can't figure her out."

They continued talking for a while until they both said that they had to go. Jack wondered what the assignment could be. He was less interested about the woman Michael had met. It sounded interesting, but he was sure that his nephew was no neophyte when it came to women. Jack knew that Michael had had an involvement with a St. Louis woman. He also was certain that it was one of convenience, his convenience. He had met her—she and Michael were not compatible mentally. He was thinking about going to Brussels to visit Michael. The legal practice was in a bit of a seasonal lull—nothing that couldn't wait a few days or be handled by one of his junior associates. Also, getting away from Lynn Massey Gallagher would be more than welcome. He hadn't been to Brussels in a while. The phone call he received a bit later cemented the Brussels visit.

CHAPTER 11

ABU AWAMI ORGANIZATION IN THE PNZ

Mike Burdick thought he should corner Bill Arthur sooner rather than later, as the party at Arthur's house was now at a decibel level that indicated that the crowd was getting to the point where sobriety would soon be a casualty. Mike knew that Bill Arthur was always under control, but, by the look of George Padgett, Padgett was entering "twilight" zone. George's wife, Renée, was obviously trying to get George to curtail his drinking.

Burdick edged his way over to where Arthur and his wife were holding a gab fest with several Getty people. The conversation seemed to be about where the couples would go when their "extended vacation" time was reached. Because of the hardship associated with working in the Zone, all employees received what was called "long leave," which, for most, was a six week minimum annual vacation. Mike excused himself and apologized for the interruption but muttered that he was here for a short time and needed to talk to Bill Arthur. Arthur took Burdick to an unoccupied corner of his house.

"Bill, I have two things I want to talk to you about. One is sort of personal—it has to do with the overlap between you and George Padgett. The other has to do with the intrusion this morning at

Ghanem's office by some thugs who Hassan told me were Abu Awami and his gang. Quite frankly, they scared the crap out of me. Hassan said they didn't represent a threat to Americans. What gives?"

Bill smiled and poured himself and Mike two glassfuls of Johnny Walker Black from his private reserve of alcohol. "Mike, first of all, congratulations on your deal with us—well, I mean with Ghanem. This is newfound money for us. I don't know what took us so long to figure this out, but we did, and we all are going to benefit. This is a real win/win/win.

"Next, as you know, I worked directly for J. Paul in London until he told me to get down here and run the operation. That was eight years ago. George Padgett had been in charge of the Zone from the start. Eight years ago, George's wife Mary died. George was heartbroken, I think mostly because he believed she would have lived if she had received proper medical care in the States. She wouldn't leave George for any reason. She gambled with her life and obviously lost. George took her back to Ventura to bury her and decided to retire and live in the Ventura area. Even though J. Paul was a real miser, he did have a large sense of loyalty to those who supported him, especially in the early days. George started the Getty Kuwait operation and, with help from Klaus von Bulow, handled the PR with the world's investment community. So George left with J. Paul's blessing. As one would have guessed, back in Ventura, George was literally a 'fish out of water.' Old friends had either moved away or moved on. Finally, George asked Getty if he could go back to the Zone to work. J. Paul was loyal and agreed, as long as I had no problem with having George work for me. I didn't have a problem at all—the Zone faced many problems both operationally and with coordination with the Saudis. I needed all the help I could get, and there was no one more qualified. My management style left no room for egocentric boosting."

"So," said Mike, "you and George became a team."

"Exactly! And look at the results."

"Enough said," mouthed Burdick. "It's commendable when people behave as adults. Thanks for indulging me. Now, what's the deal with George and his new wife, Renée Caspar?"

Arthur grasped Burdick's arm. "Mike, it just proves that there is a God. Your newfound friend Hassan Salam is at least partly responsible for that."

"What?" said Burdick.

"Renée is French, obviously, and is also a famous portraitist in the Arab world. She had been introduced to the Saudi and Kuwaiti Royal families and received commissions to do the portraits of most of these families. As you can see, not only is she truly a gifted artist, but she is also a true ten. She found that the social life in Kuwait City was not just superior to that in Saudi Arabia, but she also quite enjoyed it. Kuwaitis, at least the royalty and the very rich, were very liberal and had a wealthy, almost European, lifestyle. And her commissions would have her spend lengthy periods of time with her clients posing for her."

"Okay, I can understand that, but where does Hassan come into this, and how did George fit into this?"

"I'll give you what I and others think—you can believe it or not, but it is a logical explanation that most of us subscribe to. Hassan is Lebanese and came from what some say was an influential family before the civil war transformed that country from 'France' on the Mediterranean to a Palestinian terrorist state. As you may have observed, Hassan is a bit effeminate. After Lebanon literally blew up, Hassan needed a job and found one as a secretary and driver for Getty in the PNZ. Hassan fit in well with, let's say, the elite Kuwaiti and expatriate party set. As a driver, Hassan had access to a car and indeed spent much time driving the ladies of the Getty camp. It was there that he met Renée. Hassan was George's secretary and driver. Being the kind-hearted soul that he is, he introduced Renée to George. For a variety of reasons, including that she liked, if not loved, George, they got married."

Burdick liked the story and hoisted his drink to a toast to Renée and George.

"Well, good—good for both of them. Now, what's the deal with the Abu Awami gang? Hassan said they were no threat to Americans. They seem like hoodlums to me."

"Mike, they are worse than hoodlums. They are Palestinian terrorists—not the only Palestinian terrorist gang, but perhaps the worst. They kill Israelis and Palestinians who are friendly or sympathetic to the Israelis. They come here to blackmail the Kuwaitis and the Saudis: pay up, and we will leave you alone. The Saudis and Kuwaitis find it more efficient just to pay. They have plenty of money, so it's just practical. Additionally, they don't stay here very long or often. Hassan can provide you with more detail. He knows those scumbags."

"Bill, I'll have plenty of time to talk to Hassan on the drive back to Kuwait City. I think I have imposed on your hospitality enough. I'll say my good-byes to Morris, Peretti, and Ted Collins. With this deal to deliver your crude excesses via Ghanem's Tug and Barge Operation, I'll be here to make sure it gets off the ground and stays that way," said Burdick.

They both had a laugh at the phrase "Ghanem's Tug and Barge Operation." They all understood the way Getty's contracts worked with the Saudi contractors. They were pure political ploys to keep the Saudi populace happy. And they were happy making money, no matter who really did the work. All parties were happy—Getty got the needed crude, the Saudi contractors got a no-risk piece of the action, and the Getty workers got paid and paid well.

Burdick said his good-byes to the Getty people. They had known each other through a number of operations in the U.S., Canada, and the U.K. They liked each other and had respect for each other's professional capabilities. These were long-term plays, and working with people one respected and liked made life much more pleasant. Burdick had a good idea how this party would wind up, so it was time to go. Burdick said his good-byes and walked outside where Hassan was waiting.

"Hassan, let's go. I have lots of questions for you. I know you will have lots of answers."

"Mr. Burdick, I think I know what you want to find out. It's about the Abu Awami Organization. I do know a lot, and it will be my pleasure to tell you what I know. You are a friend."

The drive to Kuwait City would be long, and Burdick wanted to hear what Hassan could tell him about the Abu Awami Organization. Burdick took the seat next to Hassan in the front seat—he needed to listen to Hassan. He didn't want Hassan to take his eyes off the road to talk to him. The Middle East practice of subordinate to superior dominance would have to take the back seat, at least on this leg of the journey.

Burdick, as most American and Canadian residents, was aware of the Palestinian terrorists and the killing of Israelis by these terrorists groups. He fundamentally understood the foundation of the modern Jewish state of Israel. The Arab Nation precipitated terror against the Israelis and began wars against Israel. All of these wars, however, resulted in not just defeat for the Arabs but also humiliation for the Palestinians, who, in their minds, were the rightful inhabitants of the land called Palestine. The Jews took their land and homes. There could be no peace or accommodation with the Jew. All he knew for sure was that the Palestinian Liberation Organization (PLO) was terrorists. They had completely screwed up Lebanon and ruined what was a prosperous country and what was the region's banker and commercial entity.

He did know that there were various Palestinian terrorist organizations, and the Abu Awami Organization had the reputation of being the worst. Why, he had no clue—hopefully, Hassan would be able to shed some light on this. For Burdick, this was nearly academic, as the Palestinian terror groups, including the PLO, were not a threat to the American operations in Kuwait and Saudi Arabia. In his mind, the biggest potential threat to the American interests in the gulf would be Saddam Hussein. The Iraqis were still in the midst of a prolonged war of attrition against Iran, a war the West hoped would be long drawn out.

"So, Hassan, what is the Abu Awami Organization, and do Americans in Kuwait and Saudi Arabia really care about this group? Is it better or worse than the PLO?"

"Mr. Burdick, Americans need not fear the Abu Awami Organization in Kuwait and Saudi Arabia. They wouldn't dare touch an American here. But, to answer your question regarding the Abu Awami Organization and the PLO, I can say these groups are very different. The PLO, I detest. The PLO was largely responsible for the destruction of Lebanon. Because of the PLO, many friends and family and I had our lives uprooted and ruined. Like me, they had to leave to survive. I am in Kuwait because of the PLO, not because of Abu Awami. The Abu Awami Organization is comprised of terrorists and killers, but they only kill Israelis and Palestinians who collaborate with the Jews."

Hassan began his recitation about the Abu Awami Organization. "The Palestinian War began on November 29, 1947, when the United Nations resolved to partition Palestine into two states—one Jewish, one Arab. Fighting broke out immediately between Arab and Jewish militias. The Arabs expected an easy victory, but the Israelis soundly defeated them, as the Israelis have in every 'war.' The Arab nations refused to accept the UN partition.

"The Abu Awami Organization was just one of the terrorist groups, but it was the most prolific in terms of killing Jews and the Palestinians who would make a deal with the Israelis. The ANO ceased to exist when Abu Awami was killed in 1991, but that didn't end the conflict—just look at the PLO today, Syria, and, now, Iran."

Burdick listened to Hassan's recitation about the Abu Awami Organization with a mixture of disbelief, contradiction, and amazement. He understood that Hassan had a photographic memory, but, still, it was unbelievable that this terrorist group could have survived as long as it has. Personally, Burdick could care less about these Palestinian terrorist groups, including the PLO. It was apparent to him that the funding of these groups came largely from the Saudis and the Kuwaitis. He could basically understand why they funded these groups— as good Muslims, they had an obligation to destroy Israel. To Burdick, this was a side show and a minor one for the Saudis and Kuwaitis. Iran played a big role in the funding, as its desire to annihilate Israel was paramount.

He could understand why Israel, more so than the Saudis, Kuwait, and the other Arab nations, would want to eliminate the Abu Awami Organization and other Palestinian terrorist groups. Abu Awami and these other Palestinian terror groups killed Jews indiscriminately. He thought that because the U.S. was an unequivocal ally and supporter of Israel that America would do what was necessary to help Israel destroy the Palestinian terrorist groups, including the Abu Awami Organization. He didn't see any evidence that the PLO would be negotiating with Israel for a two-state solution in good faith at any time.

"Hassan, your memory is outstanding. You have given me an understanding of the Palestinian terrorist groups and, in particular, the Abu Awami Organization. There are a number of things I don't understand and probably never will, but after the partition by the United Nations, why didn't the Palestinians and their Arab allies simply make a deal with Israel and carve out a home for both groups as outlined by the U.N.? Instead, they went to war and lost and continued to lose."

"Mr. Burdick, you have to understand the Arab mind to answer that question. The Arabs believed that they would defeat the Jews, largely because they had the much greater numbers, and, in their heads, they were superior warriors and fighters. It is Arab pride, which is not based on reality but on myth. They still believe that they will conquer. This not only ignores the fact that Arabs are not militarily competent but also that the United States will support the survival of Israel militarily and logistically.

"It is said that an Arab has many houses he occupies in his mind, so many that he never knows which one he is in. In contrast, the Western mind has only one house, and that house is reality."

"Hassan, you are very helpful. The reality for me, though, is I need to get on with my life. I'm going to fly to Brussels and rest up for a couple of days. When we get back to the SAS Hotel outside of Kuwait City, I'll make some phone calls to set up some meetings in Brussels."

"But, Mr. Burdick, you will come back to the Neutral Zone."

"Hassan, I'll be coming back to make sure that Ghanem's Tug and Barge System is operating, so I'll be back on a regular basis."

"Mr. Burdick, you are so funny. The only involvement by Ghanem will be when he collects a portion of the profits, because his name is on the contract. This is an American project, we all know."

CHAPTER 12

MIKE BURDICK IN BRUSSELS

Burdick checked into the Kuwait SAS after Hassan dropped him off at the Salamieh, Kuwait hotel. He felt like he had come home, even though he had been there only once before on his initial trip to Kuwait. He was warmly greeted by the Danish Assistant Manager. He thought the feeling of coming home could be attributed to the fact that this was a European environment as contrasted to the isolated Saudi Arabian experience in the Partitioned Neutral Zone, where he had spent the last few weeks. Even though they were separated by fewer than one hundred miles, he felt like he was back in the twentieth century, contrasted to the feeling he experienced in the PNZ, like it was centuries ago, or maybe it was the feeling of being isolated from the civilized world that he knew. It was as if he had been suspended in a time bubble. He had checked the bottle of Johnnie Walker Black with the hotel's baggage/parcel holding. He gave the claim check to the assistant manager, Christian Olsen. He thanked Olsen and proceeded to his room after picking up a bucket of ice. He fixed himself a drink and then called the operator and asked him to place a call to Jack Gallagher in St. Louis. He then changed into a pair of shorts and a golf shirt and stepped out onto the balcony, which overlooked the hotel's swimming pool. He sipped his drink and waited for the call to Gallagher to come through. Several lovelies were tanning themselves as the sun began its slow descent into the night. Burdick thought he might just have to wander down to have a closer view of the talent. Just then, the phone rang. It was Gallagher.

"Hello Jack, thanks for calling back. Listen, I've finished up my work here. It looks like I've sold Getty a tug and barge system. Actually, it's the system that has just come off charter. You cleared up the legal problems for me. Listen, that's not why I called. I am flying to Brussels tomorrow. I plan to spend some time in Brussels checking out the local art galleries—I understand there are some interesting sights to check out."

"Mike," chuckled Jack, "you haven't changed. But how about your new lady friend?"

"I've the feeling that she won't mind—in fact, she might enjoy my absence. Jack, I know you have a nephew who has recently been posted to Brussels. Why don't you come over and visit him? You could help me out in my, uh, sight selection. If you can swing it, I'll book you into the Conrad. I'm sure you could squeeze a few days out. Just a suggestion—your call."

"Mike, you must be a mind reader. I do want to see my nephew Michael. I'll book a flight for the day after tomorrow. Get me that room. Of course, my legal fees will be reasonable."

They both had a laugh at that before they rang off. Burdick thought he would now meander down to the pool to inspect the talent lounging about. After all, R&R meant rest and relaxation—he thought he would concentrate on the relaxation part this evening.

He left his room and went down to the front desk where Christian Olsen was still holding forth. He told Christian he had an early flight to Brussels and asked Christian to have a car to take him to the airport. Meanwhile, he grabbed a copy of the Kuwait Times, the only local paper printed in English. He knew it was heavily edited, but it was better than nothing. He didn't intend to use the pool, so he had a pair of khakis, a golf shirt, and a pair of tan loafers. He walked to the pool and stopped by the first lovely's resting place. She was Lebanese and beautiful. Their conversation was brisk and brief. She informed Mike that she was working for the Kuwaiti Deputy Minister of Education. Burdick quickly cut his losses and returned to his room after asking Christian to reserve a room at the Conrad Hotel in Brussels for him and Jack Gallagher. He returned to his room's balcony and continued his viewing of the lovelies by the pool. At least, he thought, the Kuwaiti Deputy Minister had good taste. He suspected the other pool side beauties had similar arrangements. He wasn't certain how much these "arrangements" cost the Kuwaiti Government, but it was certainly a number that would choke a horse.

He sipped his drink while perusing the Kuwaiti Times. He came across an article that caught his attention. It was a brief article that referred to the Kuwaiti Minister and Deputy Minister of Education. The article briefly stated that the Ministers would be attending a conference of Arab Nation education ministers in Athens beginning today and lasting for six days. Burdick stood on his balcony and caught the eye of the Lebanese beauty. He pointed to the Kuwaiti Times story. Shortly thereafter, there was a knock on his door. He opened the door and the waiter handed him a note. The note said that she would meet him at the Hilton Hotel in Kuwait City at 6 p.m. He looked down and signaled to her an okay. The note was signed, "Nancy Saliba."

Mike boarded KLM flight 53 for Brussels. The Dutch stewardess welcomed him and showed him to his aisle seat 3B. He thought that whoever was responsible for hiring the KLM flight crews should be given a medal. She announced that her name was Marla. She said she was on board to ensure Mr. Burdick had a pleasant and relaxing flight. She brought him a serving tray with a choice of coffee or tea. He buckled up and sat back. She took his tray as the pilot taxied the Boeing 747. An announcement over the intercom stated that they had been cleared for takeoff. The jumbo jet lumbered down the runway and, after thirty-two seconds, became airborne. They quickly reached their cruising altitude.

After a few more minutes, the pilot announced over the intercom that they were now out of Kuwaiti airspace, and the drinking light was lit. This was met with cheers from the first class passengers. Marla leaned over and asked Mr. Burdick if he would like a glass of champagne or some other beverage. Mike indicated that champagne would indeed be welcome.

"Marla, you are indeed a natural beauty and as nice as can be. I'll also have a scotch on the rocks—make it a double. Then I'll get some sleep. Please wake me when we start our descent into Brussels. You are wonderful."

She brought the drink and wished him pleasant dreams. Burdick's dream about Nancy Saliba was interrupted by Marla's pleasant voice asking Mr. Burdick to wake up. "Mr. Burdick, please wake up—the pilot has announced that we will begin our descent and will land in Brussels in twenty minutes." Burdick opened his eyes and saw that Marla was speaking to him. For an instant, he thought that Marla was an angel. He briefly muttered a thank you. He wanted to say more but was truly at a loss for words. What could he say other than "thank you."

The plane continued its uneventful descent into the Brussels International Airport. The Boeing 747 came to a stop. Marla took Mike's arm and guided him gently to the exit door while telling him she hoped to see him on another KLM flight soon. He told her that he hoped so, and he proceeded down the ramp headed for baggage claim. He retrieved his luggage after what he thought was an unusually long wait. He exited the airport and grabbed a cab. "The Conrad Hotel," he told the cabbie, who tried to sell him a roundtrip ticket, which Mike wisely declined. He was looking forward to his stay at the Conrad and seeing his old friend Jack Gallagher.

The drive into the city was pleasant. He thought the city had a pleasant layout—no high rises and unique styles of buildings, which, in his view, blended well together. This was a new experience, as he had never been to Brussels before now. The taxi maneuvered adroitly through Brussels' traffic. Burdick was impressed with the driver's skill and deportment. It was a far cry from New York cab drivers' skill and generally belligerent behavior, not necessarily to their customers but to the other drivers. The cab turned onto Avenue Louise, a tree-lined pleasant street, and then turned into the drive of the Conrad. The hotel was set back about fifty yards from the avenue. The drive was wide and had a dark gray slate surface that enhanced the approach visually. The uniformed attendants immediately greeted the cab as it stopped and greeted the passenger in four languages. When Burdick said thanks, they immediately continued in English. Burdick was impressed—the façade of the hotel was angled neatly, which was majestic. Mike knew Jack Gallagher would also be impressed.

Michael Gilmartin was attempting to focus on his incoming correspondence with little success when his phone rang. "Hello," he said. "Michael, it's your uncle Jack. Listen, I warned you I would pay you a visit soon. Well, the 'soon' is the day after tomorrow. I'll be in Brussels for four or five days. Don't worry, you won't have to look after me continuously. I'll be meeting up with Mike Burdick, an old friend and former client who will be coming in from Kuwait. We will be staying at the Conrad."

"That's great, Jack. Great restaurants here, and I'm still at the Conrad. I'll set up dinner—just call me when you get in. Oh, I'll probably bring Milledufleur Rose. I'm sure you'll like her."

"Sounds great, look forward to it."

Michael immediately called Milly Rose. He left her a message to meet him at the Conrad downstairs piano bar at 5. He also said he had some interesting news.

Michael arrived at the downstairs bar ten minutes before 5—he didn't want to miss her. He hadn't seen her since that night, the night he would never forget, ever. The piano player was already into his tunes, soft and pleasant light jazz. The bar was about half-filled, mostly businessmen but a few well-dressed and attractive women. He munched on the peanuts on the table—it was more a reflex action than any hunger. He ordered a Jameson on the rocks with water on the side. The more he thought of her, the higher his anxiety level climbed. She was like no one ever before, even in his imagination.

He was glad his uncle Jack would be visiting—after all, he was the primary motivator for Michael to join the FBI, a move he was glad he had made. He began reviewing Tom Turner's file on the Abu Awami Organization while he waited. What, he wondered, was Milly's interest in the Abu Awami Organization? Perhaps it was more than just a scholarly interest in all things Middle Eastern, but, certainly, the Palestinian/Israeli conflict was the most important aspect concerning that region currently and for a long time. As he was musing, he smelled her before he saw her. Oh my God, he thought, she is even more beautiful than he remembered. He stood as she sauntered toward the table. She smiled and mouthed a "hello" as he reached for her hand and gave it a squeeze as he kissed her cheek. He helped her to her chair. Now he was truly flustered, but she erased all qualms as she told him that it was good to see him.

She took the chair he offered and, as she sat, took his hand and gave it a squeeze. He nodded to the waiter, who had asked what he could do for the lady. Michael was sure that if he could read the waiter's mind, he would know what the waiter would like to do. Michael wondered, as he had done so in the brief time he knew her, how many men she had shared her, or their, bed with. He dismissed the thought instantly, rationalizing that it didn't matter.

"Michael, it's good to see you. It seems like only yesterday that we had that lovely dinner and had a chance to, ah, get to know each other, and I mean know each other in the biblical sense."

This had the effect that she had intended. He nearly moaned but just squeezed her hand firmly. She ran her hand on his leg as she told the hovering waiter she would have a Bombay gin and tonic. The waiter smiled and averted his eyes from the under-the-table play as he scurried away.

"Milly, my uncle, Jack Gallagher, will be in Brussels the day after tomorrow. Jack was the main reason I joined the FBI. He was an agent for six or so years before he retired and became a partner in a Clayton, St. Louis law firm. Quite a lucrative deal, but Jack also married well, at least financially. He is coming to Brussels to see me, but he also will meet up with an old pal of his, Mike Burdick. Burdick has been in Kuwait for the last several weeks. He has done a deal with a Getty Oil Saudi Arabian contractor. He told Jack that the trip was a real eye-opener. According to Jack, Burdick knows some of the top Getty people in the Partitioned Neutral Zone of Kuwait. He also told Jack he had some eye-opening experiences while he was there. I hope you will be able to have dinner with us."

Milly's interest was more than piqued. She of course was quite familiar with Kuwait and Saudi Arabian scene. This might be interesting, she thought.

"Of course I would like to have dinner with you, your uncle, and his friend. Looks like I will be outnumbered—three men and one woman. Do you think they would mind if I invited a friend?"

Michael hesitated before asking, "Who do you have in mind?"

"She is the assistant to the Dean of the University. She is Flemish, about forty, and quite friendly. Your uncle's friend might like her—she enjoys life, if you know what I mean. She also is familiar with the Middle East—her ex-husband was Lebanese, Christian Lebanese, to be exact. Her name is Kirsten Rutten—she kept her maiden name."

Michael frowned, "I'm not sure how she would fit in. The extra cost for a dinner isn't a problem. Burdick and Uncle Jack have plenty of money. Hell, even on my salary, that kind of money isn't a problem. I just don't know how they would interact with your friend Kirsten."

"Michael, it's just a dinner. I would be more comfortable with her than with just three men. Besides, she is familiar with the PLO and Palestinian terrorist activities. I'm still very interested in the activities of the Abu Awami Organization and the work your predecessor, Tom Turner, put together during his stay as Legal Attaché."

"Let's talk about that later, if at all. Right now, let's take care of the dinner. Look, I don't think Uncle Jack would care, but he isn't at all interested in what happens in the Middle East."

"But you are, I am, and, I suspect, your uncle's pal, Burdick, is, given he will be involved with Kuwait and Saudi contractors. Besides, she is very attractive, and I understand that Mike Burdick is not married."

Michael really wanted to see Jack Gallagher and show him an entertaining time in Brussels. He needed to fix this and get on to other things that were pressing to him—namely, the bedding of Milledufleur Rose. Not then, but now.

"Milly, sure. If your friend wants to have dinner, then fine."

"Good, Michael. Also, I would suggest we not have dinner at the Conrad. There is a restaurant within walking distance from the hotel named La Quincaillerie. It is popular with the local gentry. Your guests, I'm sure, will like it. As a matter of fact, I think you would enjoy it. I'm sure you haven't been there."

"I surrender. Invite your friend, and the Quincaillerie it is. Why don't we have a preview dinner there, unless you have a different idea."

Milly squeezed his hand, while rubbing his leg. "Why don't we finish our drinks, then we can go to dinner. I suggest that we have dinner at that place that you really liked. It's close, too—25 Rue Gerard. Let's hurry—there is a pre-dinner activity I can't wait to get into."

Michael Gilmartin could only nod and grab the waiter—he couldn't wait. He could just moan "on y va."

Just about the time that Michael was entering Milly for the second time since their arrival at 25 Rue Gerard, Mike Burdick was giving himself a guided tour of the Conrad hotel's lounges, bars, and restaurants. He didn't expect Jack Gallagher for several more hours. He kept thinking about Nancy Saliba and the dinner at the Hilton in Kuwait City. There was nothing unusual about the dinner except for the foreplay they had engaged in at the restaurant. She showed an interest in what Burdick was doing in the Partitioned Neutral Zone of Kuwait. She was very informed, or at least he thought she was, about Abu Awami. After her third drink of Burdick's smuggled scotch, she became more vociferous about her hatred and disgust with the Abu Awami Organization and indeed with all the Palestinian terrorist organizations, especially with the PLO.

She ascribed her current fate and the horrible state of the Lebanese people, especially the Christian Lebanese, to Arafat's occupation of Lebanon. The irony, she said, was that while the PLO was occupying

Lebanon, the PLO was condemning the Israelis for taking land that the PLO claimed rightfully belonged to the Palestinians. She was becoming more hysterical the more she drank. She exclaimed that the Israelis did nothing even close to the Palestinian people that the PLO did to the Lebanese. Because of what the PLO did, she and many Lebanese women were forced to become whores to the Arabs in order to survive.

She drank more and more, slurring her words while thanking Burdick for being a gentleman—in her opinion all Americans were gentlemen. Burdick believed he had just been given a tutorial on Palestinian terrorist organizations, especially Abu Awami. She was especially impressed that he had actually seen Abu Awami, something not many could claim. He would have been more interested in exploring other aspects with her, but the alcohol had a prior claim.

Mike helped her to her feet and guided her outside of the Hilton, where he grabbed a cab. He took her to her room at the SAS and helped her to bed. She muttered a "thanks" as he left the room.

Burdick wound up at the downstairs bar where Milly and Michael Gilmartin had begun their foreplay just hours before Burdick arrived. The piano player was still plinking the ivories as the room was now nearly at capacity. More couples and single men and women had arrived. The decibel level had increased to the point where conversations couldn't be deciphered unless one took a seat at that table. Burdick liked the atmosphere and the Conrad. He ordered a Dewar's neat with water on the side. He was relaxed and looked forward to his pal Jack Gallagher's arrival. He had never met Gallagher's nephew, but if he was anything like his uncle, they would have a great time. Burdick was impressed with the talent—it was just outstanding, in his opinion.

As he was checking his watch, one of the talents came to his table and asked if she could join him. Her excuse was that the bar was jammed and that she was expecting a friend shortly. Burdick nodded and accepted her offer to buy him a drink. He told her he was also expecting a friend, so maybe they could get to know each other. He thought she was not bad—she was well-dressed, and her English was good with a bit of a French accent. All in all, it was not a bad way to spend his time. He wondered if she was a professional or if this was going to be amateur hour.

He didn't have to wait long to find out. Her friend showed up a few minutes after the drink she had ordered for him arrived. She introduced her friend to Mike. The friend's name was Collette, and she finally introduced herself as Maria. She and her friend both ordered a glass of Chardonnay. Collette was wearing a black cocktail dress that highlighted an attractive, if not sexy, body. They told Mike that they worked together at a local bank and were out to have dinner and a few drinks. They asked Mike when his friend would arrive. He told them it should be shortly—at least, he hoped so.

Mike's newly-found friends announced that they were both single and asked Mike if he and his friend were also. Mike told them that he was single, but his friend Jack was married. Maria said that if his friend was also an American, there would not be a problem, so long as his wife wasn't with him. After all, it would just be drinks and dinner.

Mike excused himself—he wanted to check and see if his friend Jack had arrived. He took the stairs to the lobby. As he approached the front desk, Jack Gallagher was being escorted by one of the uniformed attendants. The attendant had Gallagher's luggage in hand, much to Mike's relief.

"Jack," exclaimed Mike, "it's great to see you! How was the flight?"

"Mike Burdick! It was good—I managed to sleep most of the way. A little jet lagged, but feeling pretty good all in all. I'll check in and freshen up. Where will you be?"

"There is a bar downstairs. I have a table that is currently being guarded by two of the local lovelies. The place is packed. I've saved you a spot."

Jack laughed, "Burdick, you old reprobate, you haven't changed a bit. I'll be down in a flash. I need to phone my nephew, Michael Gilmartin, and at least leave him a message."

"Great, you can't miss me. The bar is jammed, but it's not that big. Just look for me with two lovelies."

Mike returned to the downstairs bar where his new friends, Collette and Maria, were indeed saving a space for him and his newly-arrived friend. Collette and Maria greeted him like a long-lost friend. They both embraced him and kissed him in the French manner—a small buss on both sides of his cheek. Well, he thought, things are looking up.

"Ladies, thanks for saving a chair for my friend and me. He is in and will be down in a few minutes. Meanwhile, let's talk about what you would like to do tonight. I am told there are several good restaurants in the hotel. How does that sound to you?"

Collette and Maria looked at each other and both shrugged their shoulders as if to indicate, what the hell? Maria said, "Why don't we wait until your friend joins us? Then we can decide."

"So," Mike said, "you want to check him out before you even commit to dinner."

Maria spoke up, "No, we don't need to check him out. You already told us that he was better looking than you, so we think he will meet our standards, as high as they are. We just want to talk to both of you about what your expectations are for tonight."

Mike smiled and said, "Sounds good. I can't tell you what Jack's looking for, but I know what mine are—eat, drink, and be merry. How about that?"

Collette and Maria began conversing in French, which left Burdick clueless. His language skills were primitive, at best. He could distinguish French from Greek, but that was the extent of his competence. They were speaking rapidly while giving him a smile. They would then continue in French with more chuckles and, what he thought, knowing glances in his directions.

Maria finally switched the conversation to English and apologized to Mike for being rude. She told Mike that they were talking about a mutual friend of theirs and that it had nothing to do with him. As they were explaining, Jack Gallagher walked into the bar. He spotted Mike and his two friendly's and quickly headed through the smoke to where they were perched.

Maria said to Collette, "Il est beau." Collette nodded and said, "C'est ca." Mike figured that they liked Jack's looks.

Mike introduced his new friends Collette and Maria to Jack. "Jack, these friendly ladies would like to get to know us better. I suggested dinner, but I think they want to name the place."

Jack smiled at Burdick's new trophies, if they could be called that. In reasonably good French, Jack told the ladies that he was tired from the trip and would like to save it for another day. He politely asked for their phone numbers and told them that he and Mike had some important business to talk about. He escorted Mike out of the bar and navigated the ladies to the Lobby Bar.

Mike realized that he and Jack needed to talk about the agreement that he had with the Saudi contractor Ghanem al Ghanem, but they both knew the performance on Burdick's part was a slam dunk. The operation was straight-forward. The retrofit needed to transport the crude was also a no-brainer. Payment wasn't a problem, as Ghanem would be backed up by Getty. After all, the raison d'être for the trip was for Jack to visit his nephew and for Mike and Jack to have some fun chasing women and acting like the young men they were only marginally now.

They took a table at the rear of the lobby bar, which was not jammed like the downstairs bar. The lobby bar was a place where most patrons began the night, not finished it. Mike thought he had covered the chasing of women well with Maria and Collette—well, he still had the phone numbers, but the trip would be quick. Besides, Brussels presented plenty of opportunities, as far as he could tell. Mike didn't think that Jack would have interest in the exposure he had had to the Abu Awami gang in the PNZ of Kuwait. He suspected that Jack's nephew might have an interest—well, he would find out soon enough.

A waiter stopped at their table and took their drink order—Dewar's neat with water on the side. Mike didn't think Jack looked too worse for the wear—his protestations of jet lag were overstated. Maybe Jack just wanted to talk—he would find out soon.

"Jack, I know the main reason you are here is to visit with your nephew, but it does give us a chance to catch up and have some fun. This deal I have with the Saudi contractor is a life saver for me. Without it, I probably would have been wiped out financially. I don't see much risk in the deal, do you?"

"No, not from what I've seen," said Jack. "But I can't really assess the risks that would surround the deal, because you will be operating in a Middle East environment. Seems to me, though, that because it's really Getty Oil who you are dealing with, the risk is minimal. Hell, Getty has been operating there for decades. For Getty, the Saudi contractor is just a political expediency, like keeping the natives happy, which, as I understand, comes with the territory."

"That's my understanding," said Mike. "I know most of the Getty managers in the PNZ operation, especially Bill Arthur, the current General Manager, and George Padgett. Together, Padgett and Arthur have been there since J. Paul Getty was awarded the concession by the King of Saudi Arabia. Part of the deal was that the King's Saudis be taken care of with employment and training and the Saudi contractors be protected financially. As you probably know, the Saudis run a very tight security ship in Saudi Arabia and in the PNZ, which the Saudis consider a part of Saudi Arabia."

"So you don't have anything to worry about, unless the Muslim Brotherhood takes over."

"That's not even likely in our lifetime," said Mike. "What have you heard from your nephew about the dinner party he wants to have for you?"

"I don't have all the details but should later tonight. I do know that he will invite a Professor of Middle East Studies at the University of Brussels. Her name is Milledufleur Rose. I'll get the rest of the details later tonight. He says she is one gorgeous woman."

"Good for your nephew, but how about the rest of us Indians?" said Mike.

"Don't worry, old friend—you'll have plenty of time. You will be here for four days."

"Listen, let me tell you about a sort of bizarre experience I had in the PNZ. Getty assigned me a driver and translator by the name of Hassan Salam. He drove me out to meet with Ghanem al Ghanem at his so-called office in Wafra, which is a real desert hellhole. While there, Ghanem had a visit from a group of bandits called the Abu Awami Organization. These men were armed to the teeth and were raising hell and firing their weapons in the air. They seemed to be friendly to Ghanem. They scared the hell out of me, but Hassan and, later, Bill Arthur told me that they wouldn't harm Americans. They, in essence, blackmail the Saudis and Kuwaitis, who pay up willingly. During the trip back to Kuwait City from the Getty installation at Mina Saud, Hassan gave me a tutorial on this Palestinian terrorist gang."

Jack shook his head and wondered where Burdick was going with this. "So, Mike, what does all of this have to do with what we are doing? I'm meeting up with my nephew, and we're having dinner with his professor friend and some others." Jack stopped abruptly and stared hard at Burdick. "Oh, crap, how dumb am I? Michael is an FBI Legal Attaché and, as such, liaises with the host country Belgium and the representatives of NATO and the EU. He told me he had an interesting assignment but then hushed up. And his friend, a Professor of Middle Eastern Studies at the University of Brussels, would be at least aware of the Palestinian Liberation Organization and the various Palestinian terrorist groups. I guess I've been too isolated in the west end of St. Louis County and clipping coupons to realize that there is a dangerous neighborhood out there called the Middle East. Outside of the fact that we get most of our oil from there and the Palestinians are waging constant conflict with a U.S. ally, Israel, I'm more concerned with how the St. Louis Cardinals are playing than with the operations in the Middle East. The oil keeps flowing, and Israel is doing more than holding their own in their neighborhood against the Arab nations, so what's the problem?"

"Well, Jack, you aren't alone. Until I rubbed shoulders with some Arabs and talked to the guys at Getty's PNZ operation, I never gave it much thought, other than reading an occasional article about Israel or OPEC in the Wall Street Journal."

"Mike, this dinner tomorrow night has suddenly taken on a significance that simply wasn't there yesterday."

"So, right now, I will have to spend time in the Middle East in order to complete the contract with Getty—it's a vested interest now. Even if your nephew is living in Brussels, it looks like he will be involved with what happens in the Middle East. Maybe that old expression 'it's a small world' has some significance now."

They continued talking while sipping their drinks. Their conversation then drifted to dinner and where they might go. Suddenly, two new patrons entered the Lobby Bar. It was Burdick's two "lovelies," Collette and Maria, who were heading straight to Jack and Mike. "Well, you two, how about having dinner with us at Chez Leon? It's nearby, and we have a reservation. And since you lads are new to Brussels, the atmosphere at Chez Leon will do more than dining at the Conrad will. While the food is excellent at the Conrad, the ambiance at Chez Leon will show you what you can expect in the many restaurants and bars in Brussels."

Mike looked at Jack and shrugged as if to say, why not? Mike said, "It's your call, but we're going to have dinner somewhere—why not with these two?"

Jack picked up the conversation and told Collette and Maria to lead on and that they would follow. Collette and Maria took the Americans' arms and marched them out of the Conrad. They walked together for several blocks, turned west, and entered an area that could only be called interesting. Chez Leon was one of the more interesting facades. They entered the café and were promptly greeted by a smiling maître d, who introduced himself to the gentlemen as Charles. To the ladies, he bowed and said, "Welcome back, ladies."

Charles bid the group to follow him, as he led them to a table for four in the dimly lit café. The clientele appeared to be mostly business men still in their office garb, while the women seemed to be out for a good time with men who were not their husbands. It was clear that the females were not professionals. Burdick asked their female companions of the moment if they would like a drink before dinner. Each woman ordered a glass of Chardonnay, while

Jack and Mike continued drinking Dewar's on the rocks with water on the side. Charles left menus for the group and announced that their special for the day was Dover sole, fresh off the boat. He then scurried away to fetch their drinks.

Charles brought the drinks quickly and then asked if they had any questions about the menu selection, to which they mouthed a "no merci." Mike proposed a toast before asking the ladies a question. "You are both attractive women—why did you go to such length to go after us tonight?"

Answering for both of them, Maria said, "That's simple, mes hommes. First of all, you are both attractive men, but maybe, more importantly, it's because you are Americans."

Burdick said, "What, because we're Americans? That's a new one for me—how about you, Jack?" Jack nodded in agreement.

Maria took the question. "It's actually pretty simple, at least to us. It's because Americans are gentlemen. You may not have noticed, but among the male clientele, there are many Germans and, what is more offensive, there are a number of Arabs, particularly Lebanese and Palestinians. They treat women roughly—we all have had bad experiences. While some of the Palestinians have the same complexion as you, they are actually terrorists visiting Brussels—the PLO type."

Collette added, "There has been an influx of Palestinian terrorists into Brussels and Belgium in recent years. There is an apparent connection between Brussels and Poland, where Allawi al Otaibi, who people say is Abu Awami, has a hide-out in the countryside of Warsaw. He has been spotted in a number of bars and cabarets across Brussels."

Burdick nearly choked on his drink when Collette mentioned "Abu Awami." "Jack, that is the guy that I encountered in Kuwait. Hassan Salam of Getty gave me quite a lot of information about Abu

Awami and the other Palestinian terrorists groups. Seems like they kill only Israelis and Palestinians who cooperate with the Israelis. Very frightening, even if they don't go after us."

Maria added, "Abu Awami and his group have had some encounters with friends of ours. They have a very bad reputation— they are mean and treat women harshly."

"So, we Americans have a reputation of being nice. That doesn't mean we would turn down a chance to sleep with one of you lovely Belgian women."

"No," said Collette, "that is the point. It would be mutual and with no recriminations after."

Burdick took Maria's hand and asked her if she wouldn't mind if they could get together after dinner. She laughed and said, "Peutetre," which Mike took as a definite maybe.

CHAPTER 13

DINNER WITH MILLEDUFLEUR

Burdick was finishing his dinner as he took Maria's hand once again. Jack Gallagher was getting ready to exit Chez Leon. Jack told Mike that he was going to get a cab for Collette. He told Mike he would see him back at the Conrad for a nightcap. Burdick, however, was still operating on his "definite maybe" from Maria. Mike picked up the dinner tab and was profusely thanked by all, including Jack.

Jack and Collette left the restaurant while Mike was still fiddling with the tab. He definitely had the intention of trying to make a night of it with Maria. He finally settled the bill for their dinner. He escorted Maria from the restaurant.

"Let me get a cab and take you home," said Burdick.

"That's nice of you, but you don't have to take me home. I've a long day tomorrow, and it's late. I need to go to bed—alone," she emphasized.

While they were talking, a car pulled up, and four men got out. Burdick recognized the older of the group with a balding pate and a mustache. "My God" he exclaimed while pointing to him, "that's the guy I ran into in Kuwait's PNZ, the one they call Abu Awami!"

Maria clutched Mike's arm and said in a tone just above a whisper, "We've seen him and his friends several times in clubs of the area. They are Palestinians and have been very mean to several of our friends. I didn't know their names, but I know how dreadful they behave. Let's get a cab and get out of here, now!"

Burdick was certain that the short balding man was the man who he encountered outside of Ghanem al Ghanem's place in Wafra—Abu Awami. The other men with Abu Awami were Isami Marzan, deputy chief, Abdallah Hassan, head of the committee for Revolutionary Jihad, and Hashem Harb, a key man in their foreign operations. Burdick didn't know their names, but he recognized their faces from the encounter at Ghanem's place in Wafra.

Maria and Burdick jumped in the cab called by the Chez Leon's maître d'. Maria gave the driver her address. Burdick thought he might just luck out after all. They quickly arrived at her apartment. Burdick paid the cab fare and exited the cab. Maria told the driver to wait, as her dinner companion would be returning to the Conrad Hotel.

"Mike, thank you so much, but, as I said earlier, I need to call it a night. Besides, I think we've both had enough excitement for one night. But I could meet you tomorrow for drinks or for dinner."

Burdick muttered a profanity to himself. He wondered if he could be bold enough to invite Maria to dinner tomorrow. What the hell, he thought, why not? After all, it's just dinner.

The four Palestinians went into the Chez Leon, where they were warmly welcomed by the club's proprietor and staff. The proprietor and staff then ushered these four men to a private room. The Palestinians told the waiter that they wanted drinks and dinner. They emphasized they wanted to be served quickly and then left alone, as they had some private matters to discuss.

As they had requested, the drinks and dinner arrived quickly. Allawi al Otaibi (Abu Awami) told the waiter to keep the drinks coming but to knock before entering the room. The group represented the top echelon of planning and execution of the Abu

Awami Organization. At the meeting were Allawi al Otaibi, the leader of the group and the head of the ANO Political Bureau, Isani Maraqa, deputy chief of the Political Bureau, and Abdallah Hassan (Abu Nabil), the head of the committee for Revolution Jihad. From the Revolutionary Council were Hishan Harb, key man in foreign operations, and Sami Abu Ali (Mazen-Khalili), People's Army Directorate. Majid Al-Akkawi, the Deputy Head of People's Army in Northern Lebanon, was invited and was expected to attend, but he had problems with his passport, which prevented his attendance at what Allawi al Otaibi called an important operations meeting. "Important operations meeting" was code for who they would kill next.

Abu Awami slouched in his chair, making him look even smaller than he was. He proposed a toast to the liberation of Palestine from the Jewish oppression. "Three of our brothers are in jail in the U.K. for the attack we conducted on the Israeli Ambassador Argov to the U.K. Although Argov will never walk again, Allah allowed this Jewish pig to survive. We must be careful to not allow that to happen in our next mission, which will be soon. Maintaining our manpower levels is critical. We can't play a numbers game against the Jew." This produced murmurs from the group. Abu Awami, known for his heavy drinking at night, stood and raised his glass to his brothers, draining his glass. He opened the door and demanded the waiter to bring more whiskey.

"I have killed British diplomats in Athens and Bombay, but we don't need to kill any more Brits. Our strength lies in our planning capability and in our efficient killing of the Jew and of the misguided and treasonous Palestinians who collaborate with the Jew. We have worked the Brussels connection very efficiently. By judiciously spreading our money around, we have made many friends in Brussels and indeed in Belgium. Money is not our problem—the

Saudis and Kuwaitis will supply our operation. While he doesn't have that kind of money, Saddam Hussein is generous, and so is Gadaffi—our manpower is our problem. Our end game, as you all know, is the liberation of Palestine. It is a numbers game. The Jew can be eliminated. If the Germans could have prevailed another year in the war, Eichmann would have eliminated the Jew."

Hishan Harb whispered to Sami Abu Ali, "Sometimes I wonder if he really believes that or if he is in it for the money and the blood."

Harb shook his head in agreement. Abu Awami asked if Hishan and Sami would like to share with the rest of the group. Sami spoke up, "Hishan was just saying that he agreed that this could be done, but we will need the help of the Arab and Muslim world."

Abu Awami nodded in agreement. "The Shah is very vulnerable and will be overthrown by the Mullahs in Iran. When that happens, our quest will be speeding to fulfillment."

Abu Awami walked to the door and summoned the waiter to bring more whiskey.

"Now, let us discuss the objective of this meeting. We all know the purpose of the meeting—it is to select the Jews we will kill next. Who has the names or groups of individuals who we should put on the extermination list?"

Sami said, "In my opinion, it should be prominent members of the Mossad."

Abu Awami rejoined, "Exactly, we are in agreement. Specifically, we should put two members of the Mossad on the list. One is here in Brussels, and the other will be visiting her shortly in Brussels."

"Who will we add?" said Sami. "I think we all know and agree who will be added for elimination. We will eliminate the number two man in the Mossad, its chief recruiter, Kim David, and his agent, Milledufleur Rose, who is now a visiting Professor of Middle East Studies at the University of Brussels."

The other three proclaimed their agreement with the choices. Hishan Harb asked, "When?"

Abu Awami said, "I have reason to believe that it may be sooner than later. Our intelligence believes there is a sex interest between David and Rose." Looking at Sami, he said, "Like the relationship you have with one of the ladies at the Bank of Brussels."

Sami laughed, "You do know everything."

Abu Awami, while smiling, said, "It will serve you not to forget."

The meeting/dinner/drinking session continued for some time, as Abu Awami wanted to continue the planning and the drinking. The alcohol loosened the tongues of the ANO group. They went over the options of eliminating M. Rose and Kim David. The key to elimination was when Kim David would visit Milledufleur in Brussels. They knew where Milledufleur worked and where she lived. They were also quite aware of her interest in the young American FBI Legal Attaché, Michael Gilmartin. The parole touched on the young American, and they all concluded that they would not have any involvement in any action against Gilmartin. They were all in agreement that nothing would warrant any action against the Americans. Their intelligence was good, and, even though Gilmartin had the files on ANO operations from his predecessor, Tom Turner, they were not interested in expanding their operations to infuriate the Americans. Gilmartin was on their no-touch list.

The planning session then was directed at how they could accelerate a visit by Kim David to Brussels. They discussed the effect killing M. Rose could have on drawing David out, and they concluded that it would be of no effect. They needed Milledufleur as the entrapment for David. They knew that Milledufleur was Jewish and an agent for the Mossad, but the Jew they wanted above all others at this time was Kim David. If they could use her to set up more Israelis and David, that would be a good move. While they were confident that David would visit Brussels, they needed to know when and who else would be in his entourage. Their sources/ informants informed them that there was more than a likely chance that Milledufleur Rose and Michael Gilmartin were involved in more than just a hand-holding relationship. The session evolved into a brainstorming session of how they might be able to use Gilmartin to help them in finding firmer dates as to when Kim David would visit Brussels.

Milledufleur had finished her lectures for the day and walked to her flat at 25 Rue Gerard to relax and get ready for the dinner tonight. She knew that Michael was really looking forward to having this dinner with his Uncle Jack, who Michael very much looked up to. She more than suspected that Michael insisted on her presence so that he could show her off to his uncle and to others as a trophy date, if not catch. This was just a part of her job, and she enjoyed it. So far, Michael pleased her, even if she hadn't loosened his tongue about his colleague Turner's work on Abu Awami. She wondered how much more Turner had on the Abu Awami Organization than the Mossad had. She understood that you could never have too much information in this dangerous game.

She brewed herself a pot of tea—it was too early for a glass of wine. She expected that this would be a long night. From what Michael had told her, his Uncle Jack's friend, Mike Burdick, was quite a drinker, and, apparently, Uncle Jack wasn't a novice at the game. She hadn't known Michael that long, but she observed that he had almost a hollow leg. Her friend Kirsten wasn't exactly a teetotaler, so, all in all, it had the promise of being an interesting and long night. She went to her kitchen and poured a cup of tea. She turned on her radio in the living room and tuned in the BBC. Her thoughts went to Kim David—it had been too long since she had seen him. Her thoughts drifted back to that night in London when he had called her, seemingly out of the blue, and had asked her to meet him at the Menage a Trois night club. Just thinking of that night made her moist and ache for him. She had had many encounters, but they were all for her satisfaction. It was different with Kim—she wanted to please him, and the result was an emotion she hadn't had before or since. She wanted to see him, soon.

A news flash interrupted the BBC soft music hour. The announcer, in his clipped British tones, told the audience that two Israeli diplomats were shot and killed that afternoon in Berlin. A Palestinian terrorist group announced that it had executed the oppressors of the Palestinian people. Milly uttered "merde" to an empty room. When will this killing ever stop, she wondered. She reasoned it could stop tomorrow only if the Palestinians would accept the UN-sponsored partitions giving both the Palestinians and the Jews autonomy and a homeland. Arafat had been given deals that would assure the Palestinians a country of their own. He took it to the brink, but, in the end, he rejected the settlement, and the Palestinian terrorist groups continued to kill. She sighed and, for an instant, despaired before pulling herself together—she knew that Israel would never give up. There was no other way to assure that Israel's people would survive.

Her thoughts then turned to tonight's dinner. She believed she needed to have Michael Gilmartin's confidence and use her sexual enticement as a quid pro quo to have Michael give her Jerry Turner's file on Abu Awami. She didn't think she had much time; Michael was not going anywhere in the short term, but she had the feeling that the time to eliminate the Abu Awami Organization was now. Now, before these terrorists could attack senior members of the Mossad.

Michael had told her a lot about his Uncle Jack—she felt that she almost knew him. He was almost an older, wiser brother to Michael.

Michael had told her that his decision to join the FBI was largely due to the influence of his uncle. She thought that by pleasing his uncle, she might be able to somehow get Michael to deliver at least the content of the FBI's file on Abu Awami. Kim David had stressed to her how important it was to eliminate Abu Awami and all of the Palestinian terrorist groups. She believed that Israel would have to carry this struggle for a very long time.

She had many reasons to select the Quincaillerie, not the least of which being the location. It was just off Avenue Louise, a short walk from the Conrad hotel. The restaurant was founded in the early 1900s and was indeed a hardware store until it was purchased and opened as a restaurant. The tables were located up a flight of stairs from the entrance. There were tables on the first floor, but the most prized were the tables upstairs. The stairs to the second floor led to a three foot diameter antique clock. Tables were located on either side of the divide. From that vantage point, the diners could see all of the people who came into the restaurant. There were fourteen tables, four on either side of the stairway. Even though there were only five people invited for the dinner, she reserved the entire left-hand side of the restaurant to keep the intimate gathering private. She had dined several times at the Quincaillerie and was impressed by the décor and by the outstanding choice of courses, especially the oysters, Dover sole, and lamb dishes. The wine selection was large and selective. She thought that the wait staff was friendly, efficient, and attractively-dressed. She had requested that the service be provided by her favorite waitress, Yvonne Gustine. Yvonne was in her thirties and, by acclamation, "drop dead beautiful." She didn't know many men whose heads wouldn't be turned by Yvonne.

She didn't know very much about Mike Burdick except that he had business interests in Kuwait and Saudi Arabia. She knew he was a drinking buddy of Jack Gallagher. She didn't know what

Burdick looked like, except that Michael thought that he was his uncle's age. She did know that he would be involved in the Middle East for several years at least. Maybe this would be of interest to her and her friend Kirsten Rutten, given Kirsten's Lebanese connections. Her interest in arranging dinner was solely to ingratiate herself with Michael further so that she could gain access to the FBI's files on Abu Awami. She knew she was flying blind, but she had to try something. She couldn't disappoint Kim David. She wanted to see him so much that it was beginning to hurt. Contacting him was difficult, at best, and, right now, she had to give all of her attention to the dinner for Michael's uncle, Jack Gallagher. She was beginning to harbor some doubts about her strategy of easy sex with Michael. So far, this hadn't helped her gain access to the FBI files. She knew that she couldn't put the genie back in the bottle.

There was no doubt in her mind that Kim David fully expected that she would get the Abu Awami file from Michael. This dinner was so important; if Jack Gallagher was impressed with the affair, he could motivate Michael to share the FBI file on Abu Awami. There was no logic. If balling his ears off wasn't working, why would having a nice, or even great, dinner party for Uncle Jack produce anything different? She was flummoxed, and the dinner was just an hour away. She was really angry at herself because she had no plan. All she had was Michael's heat for her in the sack. So, she thought, what am I going to do? What is my game plan? Now, she really needed a drink. Without thinking logically, she thought that Mike Burdick might be the key to the puzzle. He has a connection to Kuwait and Saudi Arabia. Kirsten had connections in the Middle East. Maybe she could be the messenger, but why would Kirsten give a rat's ass about the FBI file? She might care only because she is aware of the Palestinian terrorist groups and the danger they present to the Jews. Kirsten isn't Jewish, but she does have property in Lebanon from her divorce settlement that could be negatively impacted if the Palestinian terrorist organizations continued their inroads into Lebanon, especially if the picture in Israel deteriorated as a result of the Palestinian terrorist gangs killing of Jews. "My God," she thought, "Burdick could be the key." She needed to talk to Kirsten and fast.

Sami Abu Ali was dedicated to the Palestinian cause and the elimination of the Jews from Palestine. He had played his part and had played it well. He believed he had the trust of Abu Awami; at least, he hoped that he had this trust for his personal survival. Over the last three years, he had killed thirty Jewish dignitaries in Oslo, Stockholm, and Brussels. Abu Awami acknowledged Sami as an efficient Jewish elimination machine. But Sami knew that he must do more. Abu Awami had told him on a number of occasions to do the arithmetic; they had to step up their efforts. Sami felt the pressure; he knew, or at least thought, that Abu Awami would eliminate him and replace him in the organization if he didn't produce.

He thought the plan that they had hatched at the meeting at Chez Leon was a big step. Eliminating Kim David and Milledufleur Rose would have an impact on the Mossad. Kim David was the best recruiter the Mossad had—he would be difficult to replace. Milledufleur Rose was the attraction to get Kim David into a vulnerable position. The efforts by the PLO, while appreciated, were not enough to achieve their objective. He knew this was not a pipe dream—it could and would happen. The Jews had stolen his family's lands and the wealth those lands had produced. They would reverse this and bring the Palestinian people back to dominance.

Sami was feeling the pressure of the moment; he didn't need Abu Awami to dial it up, as it was always there. Sami needed a drink and a sexual diversion. Fortunately, there were a number of Belgian ladies, not just pure prostitutes, who could be available for drinks and dinner. He had a long list of possible women available for his diversion. He mentally reviewed the list and settled on one. It was now 10 a.m., a good time to reach her. He walked to the desk of the drab hotel room and dialed her number.

"Bon jour, c'est the bureau d' Madamoiselle Maria deBellefroid," she answered in an almost sultry tone.

"Maria, this is Sami. It's been too long without you. When can we have dinner? How about tonight?"

"Too long? It's not even 24 hours."

"I know, but I miss you so. You do things that no one else can do. How about dinner tonight?"

She thought for a minute but remembered their last time together. She still quivered when she thought of what he did to her. "Yes, but could we make it for lunch today? I have to go to a dinner tonight with an American I met recently. I think you might be interested in the people who will be attending the dinner."

"Well, why not? Where would you like to go?"

"It's a slow day at the bank. Why don't you just come by my flat? I'll throw something together. Besides, we can get to the main attraction earlier. I may need a nap before the dinner tonight."

This was fine with Sami; he couldn't wait. He thought he might be able to pole vault to her place. He planned to be there early. He was more than interested; he needed her. What he found out about the dinner was even more interesting. Milledufleur Rose was the hostess for the party. The American, Mike Burdick. invited Maria, and he had some interesting Saudi connections. Moreover, Milly Rose was the bait for Kim David. He knew Abu Awami would be impressed.

Milly called Kirsten and told her that she would like to talk to her before the dinner tonight. Kirsten was agreeable; they could arrive at the Quincaillerie twenty minutes early. Milly left her office and started walking briskly to Quincaillerie for her meeting with Kirsten. At least, she thought, the weather for Brussels was outstanding—nearly a cloudless sky and a perfect temperature of about 20 degrees Celsius. This was in contrast to the usual cloudy, cool, and often rainy days of Brussels. She thought this might be a good omen for the dinner. She was hopeful.

As she walked, she began to put together an approach to Kirsten. It would take her about fifteen minutes to walk to their meeting place. This would be an almost open-ended approach. She thought she could make a decent argument as to why Kirsten should talk to Michael about giving her the FBI file on Abu Awami or at least letting her read it. She knew what she would tell her about why she needed the file. Basically, it would boil down to Kirsten doing a favor for Milly, a friend of Kirsten. What was open-looped was why Michael would do something for Kirsten, a woman he didn't know. It couldn't be a sexual allure or entrapment. While Kirsten was attractive, she was forty or so and not as attractive as Milly, so Milly had to argue that this would really benefit her in her position as a visiting Professor of Middle Eastern Studies at the University of Brussels. She knew this was a long shot, but it was the only shot she had. So she said to herself, "On y va."

She was beginning to regain her usual confidence. She had always been confident and in control. The Mossad and Kim David highly praised her seduction of the American oilman, Drew Cahill, in her first assignment from the Mossad. Didn't she receive the highest review for her one year training stint as a new Mossad recruit? Her evaluators wrote that she had "ice water in her veins" and could kill her targets in the blink of an eye. As she walked, not only did she accelerate her gait, but her confidence grew. She didn't know Kirsten intimately, but she believed that Kirsten's financial interest in Lebanon provided incentive for Kirsten to make the pitch to both Michael and his uncle Jack. She thought Kirsten could use her feminine wiles to make a play for Jack Gallagher—that couldn't hurt. But she thought Kirsten had to emphasize that this would be a big benefit for Milly and the university who had engaged Milly as a visiting Professor of Middle Eastern Studies. As a senior member of the University's administration, Kirsten would also benefit, as the school's reputation for being one of the world's leading experts on the affairs of the Middle East would be enhanced.

She arrived at the Quincaillerie a few minutes early, before Kirsten's arrival. Milly spotted Kirsten walking at a fast pace down the street. Milly noticed that Kirsten was indeed an attractive woman with an almost regal composure. Kirsten had been at the University several years before Milly's arrival as the visiting Professor of Middle Eastern studies. Milly knew that Kirsten had much influence with the President of the college and indeed with the faculty. Kirsten had lived in Lebanon during its heyday, before the civil war and before the PLO began destroying what had been called the Paris of the Orient. Business, especially international banking, had flourished during that heady time.

Kirsten and Milly greeted each other warmly, embracing and kissing each other on both sides of the cheek. Milly thanked Kirsten for coming early so they could talk. She greeted the maître d' and explained that the other guests would be arriving shortly and that she and Madame Kirsten would take their seats upstairs and await the arrival of the other guests. Yvonne Gustine, the waitress Milly had requested to serve the party, appeared immediately and warmly greeted Milly and Kirsten. Yvonne told the ladies that she had a very nice Chardonnay that she had chilled for the dinner and asked if they would like to have a glass. They both smiled and nodded affirmatively. Kirsten took a pack of Players from her purse and, before lighting the cigarette, asked Milly if she would like one. Milly shook her head no.

Yvonne poured the wine and smartly left the table to the two women. They toasted a cheers and took a sip of the wine. Milly was seated so that she could see the entrance. Kirsten was seated to Milly's right and also had a clear view of the downstairs entrance. Two couples entered the restaurant and were seated downstairs on the left side of the restaurant. The men were well-dressed and middle-aged; the women were very well-dressed and definitely not middle-aged.

"Kirsten, first of all, I really appreciate that you agreed to come to the party for Michael's Uncle Jack and, secondly, that you agreed to meet me before the dinner. There is no sense for me to beat around the bush—there simply isn't enough time for that. I need to ask you for a favor. You are well aware of the circumstances surrounding my appointment as visiting Professor of Middle Eastern Studies."

Kirsten took a long drag from her cigarette before replying to Milly. "Milly, remember that I was one of the biggest proponents for having you come to Brussels. We are dedicated to improving the image and reputation of the University as a fountainhead of knowledge about the Middle East. Your old tutor, Bernard Lewis, is still the most knowledgeable academic for Middle Eastern studies. He fully endorsed you in that position. We are pleased that you are here."

"That is, in a sense, what I want to talk to you about. It concerns the enhancement of the school's reputation. In addition to being the foremost authority on the Middle East, Bernard Lewis is a Jew. So am I."

"So," Kirsten replied, "what does that have to do with the price of tulips in Amsterdam?"

"This is a bit convoluted, but there is an indirect connection to your interests in Lebanon. I don't have to tell you that Beirut, once the 'Paris' of the Orient, is being destroyed by the Palestinians: both the PLO and the Palestinian terrorist groups, especially the Abu Awami Organization."

"I am aware of what is happening in Lebanon, I spent some happy years there before my divorce and before the Palestinians began destroying Lebanon."

"Kirsten, let me give you my impressions and why I am asking you to do me a favor."

"Milly, what is the favor?"

"Let me get to that quickly. As you know, Michael is an FBI Legal attaché stationed in Brussels. Brussels is important to the U.S. and to the western European governments as the city that hosts NATO and the EEC. So, this assignment is a plum for a young, ambitious person like Michael. Michael's predecessor was Tom Turner, who was in that position for nearly five years. During that time, Turner did copious research on the Abu Awami Organization. This Palestinian terrorist group, while not the only one, is the most prolific in killing Israelis. The group's objective is the destruction of the Israeli state. Michael has this file, and I want you to help me get it. He knows of my interest in having this information but is not, let's say, cooperating. The favor I am asking you for is to talk to Michael and convince him to share that file or, at least the contents, with me."

Kirsten took a sip of wine and put out her cigarette. She looked intently at Milly before replying. "Milly, I have no problem in talking to Michael, but I can't for the life of me understand why he would do something for me that he hasn't agreed to do for you. Also, what's in it for me? Why should I even think of doing this?"

"Well, for starters, you do have financial interests in Lebanon, especially in Beirut, that could be rendered worthless if the Palestinian groups are successful in taking over Lebanon."

"True, but so what? I can't see how you having that file or information would prevent the Palestinian groups from taking over

Lebanon. Besides, it looks like you have somewhat of a relationship with that Gilmartin fellow. If he won't do it for you, why in the world would he do it for me? Let's face it—you are younger and more attractive than I am."

"Kirsten, I'm not suggesting that you offer to sleep with Michael. I think that a request from you, as my friend, could help me, and the University might carry some weight with him. It may be a long shot, but, right now, it's one of the few shots I have."

"What are the other shots?"

"We could directly appeal to Jack Gallagher, Michael's uncle, emphasizing how important this would be for you. Kirsten, I hope you will do this for me."

"Milly, I will. It could even be fun. Besides, what have we got to lose? Who is this friend of Jack Gallagher, Mike Burdick?"

"I have never met him; all I know is that he and Michael's Uncle Jack are long time pals. I do know that he has a working interest with the Saudis and the Kuwaitis in the Partitioned Neutral Zone. Michael only knows Burdick as being a long time friend of his Uncle Jack. I'm not sure how he fits in, but all that Michael knows is that Uncle Jack says he is quite a character, whatever that means."

While Kirstin and Milledufleur were talking at the Quincaillerie, Mike Burdick was buzzing Maria deBellefroid's apartment. She replied on the intercom and told Burdick that she would be right down. She greeted Burdick with a hug and perfunctory kiss on his cheek. "God, you look gorgeous—I could eat you up right here. You're even better than I remember."

"Well, thanks, Mike, but I think we should save our eating for the party. Tell me again—how many people will be there?"

"There will be six including you and me. Milly is giving the party for Michael Gilmartin's Uncle Jack Gallagher. Michael is a young FBI legal attaché and, I think, is getting it off with Milly

Rose. There will also be a Kirsten Rutten, who is a friend of Milly and works for the President of the University. That fills up the lineup card."

"Mon Dieu, what is a lineup card? It must be American slang for something."

Mike took Maria's arm as he guided her toward the restaurant. "Maria, tell me about the restaurant. I've been in Brussels for such a short time—I'm clueless."

"I'll tell you about the restaurant while we are walking, but could you please quit trying to rub my bum?! The restaurant is a Brussels classic. It actually was a hardware store; that's what quincaillerie means in French. They serve fabulous seafood, oysters, clams, and a great carte d'vin."

"What is a carte d'vin?"

"It's a wine list you me'chant. Now tell me about the people who will be attending."

"I've already told you as much as I know. The only one I know is Jack Gallagher, a really good guy. I've known Jack for years, as a matter of fact. Due to his legal help, I was able to secure ownership of the integrated tug and barge system that I'm operating for the Saudi Ghanem al Ghanem."

"This Milledufleur Rose, what do you know about her?"

"Not much, except she is drop dead gorgeous."

She wrinkled her nose and said "You Americans, there is the English language and then there is the American language, which is only similar."

"This will be a small intimate gathering. I hope you won't feel out of place; you are the only one that doesn't have a tie to the others who will be there."

She smiled at Burdick, "I have a tie to you cheri, and I feel like you would like to tie into me."

"We could do that and skip the dinner."

"And disappoint your friend Gallagher? Don't be silly. Besides, I can't wait to meet this assortment of your friends."

"I can't wait till it's over and we can be alone."

"Dream on, mon ami."

CHAPTER 14

DINNER IN POLAND A. AWAMI

Abu Awami had no problem posing as Dr. Sa'id, a Lebanese international business man. It somewhat frustrated him because he found the Polish language impenetrable. His wife, Hafsa, and children had no problem learning the Polish language and, in fact, had become quite fluent. His wife referred to him only as Dr. Sa'id in others' presence. In private, his wife called him "Allawi," and his children always called him "father" in Arabic. Allawi could communicate with the Poles in Lublin in a broken, halting English accent.

Fortunately for him, his wife was present whenever a meaning full dialogue in Polish was required. Hafsa was also Palestinian; not only did she have an "ear" for languages, but also, as a young girl, Hafsa attended school in England, where she became proficient in English, German, and, later, Polish. It didn't take long for her and her children to become conversant in Polish both oral and written. What's more, Hafsa's family members were wealthy Palestinians and were at the top of what was considered, before 1948, the "crème de la crème" of Palestinian society. During that time, Abu Awami met and truly fell in love with the beautiful and talented Hafsa. The happiest day of his life undoubtedly was when their respective parents arranged their marriage. His love and respect for her only grew over the years. She was not only kind and understanding of the plight of the Palestinians since 1949 but also a charming companion and was nearly insatiable in bed.

Allawi had chosen Poland as his place of refuge from the Israelis when the Abu Awami Organization determined that Quadaffi and Sadam Hussein could no longer be considered as safe. The AAO determined that Abu Awami could use a main residence away from the battles against the Jew in the Middle East, South America, and Africa. Poland was chosen for a number of reasons, not the least of which being the AAO's belief that the Israelis would not suspect Abu Awami to be located in a remote country as Poland and, indeed, in the remote area of Lublin. Abu Awami was the heart and soul of the organization—no one in AAO knew where Allawi was located. The AAO communicated with Allawi only by way of dead-end drop-boxes and, in emergencies, an international telephone number that Allawi knew to be secure.

Allawi was happy in Lublin. He could hear the tinkling of glasses and the clatter of plates as Hafsa was preparing their evening meal. He could hear his children laughing and cavorting as they helped their mother prepare their dinner. Allawi was relaxed with his family in Lublin area of Poland. Tonight Hafsa had invited Robert Spotanski to join them in dinner. Spotanski owned a general store, including a popular butcher shop. Spotanski was a genial man and was the recipient of much of the local gossip. Spotanski's wife was a close friend of Hafsa. Spotanski's wife was away in Warsaw visiting her mother, who had been very ill and not expected to live much longer.

Robert Spotanski arrived shortly before 6 pm and was warmly welcomed by Allawi and his family. For some reason, Robert admired Allawi and considered him to be a close friend. Perhaps the aura of Allawi as an international figure interested him, as Lublin did not attract many (in fact, few) visitors, especially visitors from outside of Poland. Robert was a big man and, in his younger days, was a rugby player of some renown. This gave him the chance to travel within and outside Poland. He once visited the U.K; he found that he admired and resented the Brits in the same breath. Because he had learned English, he was able to communicate quite well with Allawi.

Robert was warmly greeted by Allawi, Hafsa, and their children. Hafsa said, "Robert, sit and relax. I know you work so hard and need to relax a bit before dinner. What have you heard from Susan?"

Robert said, "What little news we get is not encouraging. My guess is that I will have to travel to Warsaw for a funeral soon."

Allawi said, "That is a problem—we are so sorry to hear that. Listen, we know you have people working for you who will keep your shops going, but Hafsa and our children can also help you out with the shops."

"You are a true friend—thank God that you and your family decided to move to our village. Your family is here year round, but I understand that your international business doesn't allow you to live here all year round."

"Robert, you are a friend. Now sit back and relax—I've brought some of the finest vodka I could find. Let's have a drink to relax, and then you can fill me in on what is going on in our village."

Allawi poured two glasses of vodka, neat, which they downed in one large swallow.

"So, Robert," said Allawi, "what is going on in our village?"

"What goes on in our village? As usual, not much—I guess we should be happy that nothing goes on. Look at what is going on in the Middle East, especially with the Israelis and the Hezbollah. They fire some rockets at the Israelis and kill a few, and the Israelis respond by killing more attackers. The Israelis are not going to part with the lands they have acquired from the 1948 United Nations' proclamation of a Jewish nation. It seems to us here that the Israelis would accept a two-state situation—a home for both the Jews and the Palestinians. I thought the U.S. had secured an agreement on this, but, apparently, Arafat had different ideas."

It took all the control Allawi had to not launch into a diatribe against the Jews and explain to Robert that the homeland of the Palestinians has always been Palestine. Where did he think the name Palestine came from? There was no sharing of the land that he and his ancestors had lived in and nurtured for these centuries. The Jews had stolen what was rightfully the Palestinian homeland. The Abu Awami Organization was getting closer to breaking the back of the unlawful occupiers. He was quite aware of the fact that the Israelis, through the unholy Mossad, would continue to kill his people. He also knew that Abu Awami was not just the brains of the Organization but also its soul. If the Jews knew where he was, they would kill him. He had avoided being executed by the Mossad by deftly moving and, now, by hiding out in a remote section of Poland. He could no longer rely on Saddam Huessein and Ghadaffi to protect him—they had worse problems than he had. The Saudis and Kuwaitis were not about to run out of money any time soon. As long as their money lasted and he could keep killing Jews, they could achieve their objective.

He poured another vodka for Robert and himself. "This is an ideal place for my family, Robert. If I could, I would spend all my time here, but I only have one way to make the money my family needs, and that is to continue my international business. It is fortunate for me that I can come here during the summer when the demands of my business do abate."

"Your wife and children are a real asset to our community. I very much appreciate your kind offer to look after my store and shops while I am away in Warsaw."

"Robert, you are my friend—it's the least I can do. Besides, it will be easy for my wife and daughters to look after your customers and the store while you are away."

Robert finished toying with his vodka and proceeded to down the remains even as Allawi stood to pour them with another drink. Allawi couldn't help but think that the Poles had hollow legs when it came to drinking.

Robert accepted the drink offered by Allawi and nodded his head to acknowledge thanks. Robert then repeated his earlier statement that not many, if any, people visited this part of Poland, the Lublin area. He then posed a question to Allawi. "I don't mean to be blunt or offensive, but why did you relocate Hafsa and your children to Poland and Lublin of all places?"

Allawi smiled and said, "Robert, that is a perfectly logical question, and I hope I can give you a logical answer. You have been to England during your rugby-playing days—I dare say that you have some impressions of England that you reached while you were there."

"For sure," said Robert. "It was a busy, crowded place with so many people—too many people. I was more than happy to return to Lublin where the pace is slower and where I could relax with my friends and family."

Allawi smiled and said, "My reasons aren't that much different. While Hafsa is Lebanese, like me, she left Lebanon at an early age to attend school in England. Her father did business in the U.K. and sent her to English schools in Scotland and then to college in London. She had a proficiency and a love for foreign languages. She majored in English, German, and Polish. While studying at London University, she met some people from the Warsaw area who spoke highly of the quality of life in Lublin. During one of her school breaks, she and one of her Polish friends traveled to Poland

and also visited Lublin. She was very impressed with the quality of life in Lublin."

"But," said Robert, "she did return to Lebanon after her schooling in England."

"Oh, sure," said Allawi, "but the situation in Lebanon was deteriorating rapidly. Due to the civil war and Israelis' invasion of Lebanon, my wife and I became very apprehensive about raising a family there. We began discussing alternatives, and, after much talk and research, we decided that Lublin, Poland could work. While I couldn't move there full-time and still maintain my international business, I could spend much of the summer there. So, that's what we did, and my family is very happy."

"I always wondered about your decision to move your family here rather than, say, the UK or even Lebanon. It seems like this has worked for and your family. You are certainly a devoted family man. Glad you're here."

"Thanks, Robert," said Allawi, "So are we. I would be happy if Lublin stayed the same, with no changes."

Robert nodded as if in agreement with Allawi. "Who knows what the future holds, but I think that Lublin has undergone many changes since the end of World War II. As you probably remember from your history classes in primary school, thousands of Jews escaped after the Inquisition in Spain, and the diaspora made its way to Poland, where these individuals were warmly welcomed by the Polish nobility. The Polish nobility realized that the infusion of people would help Poland reach its economic potential. The Jews were a perfect match for Poland's needs. They were hard-working and knew many trades and professions, including medicine. The Jews also kept to themselves socially and were not allowed to intermarry."

"So," said Allawi, "the Jews came to Poland and prospered. But then came the War. Hitler and the Nazis started to slaughter the

Jews and even established the most horrific concentration camps and execution chambers. I understand that if the War had lasted another year, it may have seen the extinction of the Jews."

"Yes," said Robert, "that is so. Not too many went to the United States, but many did manage to immigrate to Palestine. After the War, Poland did all it could to welcome Jews. Lublin was particularly a favorite location for the Jews. You may have heard of the novel 'The Magician of Lublin,' which was written by Isaac Bashevis Singer in, I believe, 1960."

"I have heard of the book," said Allawi. "My wife has read it. She tells me that this is the second book written by Singer about Lublin."

"Your wife and children are indeed a blessing for Lublin," said Robert.

It was indeed more than ironic that Allawi, the head of the Abu Awami Organization, was able to find at least temporary sanctuary in Lublin. This move was made possible and successful because of the saturation of Jews in Poland, especially Lublin. Why would the Mossad look for Abu Awami in such a remote location with a large Jewish population? Whether by design or blind luck, he was able to avoid the Mossad, at least for the time being.

Allawi had no problem serving Robert a "nightcap" vodka. Shortly after his departure, Abu Awami received a phone call from Sami in Brussels. Sami's bank lady, Maria deBellefroid, went with one of Jack Gallagher's friends, Mike Burdick, to a dinner that was arranged by Milledufleur Rose. Sami told Allawi that Maria would be going to a dinner party given by Milledufleur Rose in honor of Jack Gallagher. Sami explained again that it was highly suspected by the group that Michael Gilmartin was Ms. Rose's paramour.

"Sami," said Adu Awami, "this isn't news. We have strongly suspected that they have been linked physically, if not romantically, so there is no bomb shell there."

"Right, but the big news is that Maria deBellefroid, the lady from the bank who I've been humping, had somehow hooked up with Mike Burdick, an old friend of Jack Gallagher, Gilmartin's uncle. According to Maria, this Burdick is quite a character. He has a business interest in Saudi and Kuwait and travels there periodically. Burdick will take Maria to the party—she wasn't invited, but Burdick will bring her anyways."

"So," said Abu Awami, "I hope there is more to this narrative to warrant making this call to me. You don't know where I am, but there is some danger that the call could be traced by the Mossad. So you better have information that is critical to our cause, or there will be consequences to you that will be most unpleasant."

"I more than understand that. I am loyal to our cause, which you so ably command, and I am committed to you and the cause with my life. Here is the information that is so critical to our cause. As you know, Gilmartin is a FBI Legal Attaché assigned to Brussels. He is in possession of a detailed study about the Abu Awami Organization that was prepared by Gilmartin's predecessor, a man named Turner. In spite of all of Ms. Rose's efforts to have Gilmartin share the report with her, he has refused. Whether or not he knows she is an undercover Mossad agent, we don't know. According to Maria, the purpose of the party was to convince Gilmartin to share the Abu Awami Organization FBI report with Ms. Rose."

"And was this successful?" asked Allawi.

"No, but what is important to our cause is that Burdick made inroads to Ms. Rose, and Maria alluded to a conversation about a near-term visit to Brussels by an important Israeli that can only be Kim David."

"That is important, Sami–stay with this and do whatever you have to in order to find out when the visit will be," said Abu Awami.

"You have my pledge—I will have Maria stay in constant contact with Burdick. Maria said she thinks that, for some reason, Burdick made a big impression on Ms. Rose. Maria says he is not a very handsome man, but he is very jovial, and people seem to enjoy him. Michael Gilmartin's uncle, Jack, and Burdick are obviously very close."

"Call me only when you have new and reliable information," said Abu Awami. And, with that, he rang off.

Allawi mulled over his communication with Sami. It seemed to him that Sami had an entry to Milledufleur and this Burdick character, who was close to Jack Gallagher. Allawi trusted his senses, and his senses told him that Sami's Maria would somehow be able to find out when Kim David would visit Milledufleur in Brussels. What a coup it will be when we are able to kill David, Allawi thought. He thought that this could be a turning point in eliminating the Israelis from his country of Palestine.

Hafsa interrupted these thoughts when she ushered their children into the den to say goodnight to Allawi. This was a ritual that Allawi relished. "Say goodnight to your father, children." She took his hand and whispered that she would be down after she had put the children to bed. She smiled at Allawi and said, "I won't be long. Please wait for me—I have something I want to discuss with you. Please save a drink for me."

He said, "For sure, my sweet. What do you want to want to talk about?"

"I want to talk about us and Lublin." With that, she walked with their children up to their bedroom.

Abu Awami wondered what it was that she wanted to talk about concerning Lublin that they hadn't already discussed. She was the one who discovered Lublin and secured their home there. She and the children were solid in Lublin. He was happy here, even if three months were all he could stay each year. He was still pondering the situation when she came down from the children's bedroom.

She looked at Allawi with an intensity that he had never seen. Sure, he thought, their lovemaking did not compare with the frequency and enthusiasm it had even a year ago, and it was certainly not comparable to the intensity that their lovemaking had had after their arranged marriage. He thought that this was normal, natural. He knew that that was the reason that many of his associates had taken mistresses and prostitutes, who were not Muslim—their wives just were not as appealing as they had been. He also knew that wasn't the situation in his case. Hafsa was much more attractive than he was—he could look in a mirror and recognize that as a fact. He knew he was rather short, balding, and not handsome. He believed that she was primarily attracted to his political activism— he was much like Arafat, except Allawi was intent on a return to an all-Palestinian state. Could it be that she had taken a lover? No, he quickly dismissed this thought. While a man could be a good Muslim with more than one wife, even up to four at one time, or even sleep with prostitutes, it was haram for a Muslim woman to have sexual relations with a man other than her husband. After all, it is in the Koran as revealed by the prophet Mohammed. He was puzzled—what did she want to talk about, us and Lublin?

She took a seat in a wingback chair across from Allawi. As she sat, he stood and went to the counter and poured himself another glass of vodka. She shook her head slightly in disapproval, but this was an often-repeated occurrence that she felt she had to tolerate, as he had the pressures of raising money and advocating for a Palestinian country.

"So wife, what is it you want to discuss about our family and Lublin?" he said. "I thought you were happy here."

"We, the children and I, are happy here, very happy. It is you and your relationship with Lublin that I want to talk about."

CHAPTER 15

AN AMERICAN-POLE VISITS LUBLIN

Dave Nogalski had been planning this vacation for as long as he could remember. Dave was born shortly after his parents had immigrated to Chicago from their native Poland. He and his Polish-American friends all had heard the same stories about Poland, the good and the bad. There were more Poles than any ethnic nationality in Chicago. The Poles outnumbered even the Irish, Italians, and Germans. They had assimilated into the American fabric like most of the other ethnic groups who had immigrated to America had. They were Americans who happened to have Polish roots.

Dave was 43 years old and had recently experienced severe changes in his life. He had been married to Mary Ryan for eighteen years before she had passed away from cancer of the uterus. They didn't have children, even though they had both wanted a family. Dave was the CEO of a Chicago-based industrial minerals company. Before Mary became ill, he had taken almost no vacation or personal time from the job. He was sure he would never recover from Mary's death. He heeded his friends and family's urging to take some time off and rebuild his life. He had many Polish-American friends, some of whom had visited Poland. It was these friends that convinced him he should go to Poland, especially to Lublin.

Lublin had a history that interested Dave. He knew people who had spent time in Lublin, and their stories and recollections about the Lublin history and people fascinated him. He had very little comprehension of the Polish language but was assured by his friends that he would be able to cope, as most of the Poles spoke English. This was especially true of the Polish Jews who were nearly exterminated by the Nazis. The Polish people and government had implemented programs to encourage the immigration of Jews into Poland. This was especially true of the Lublin area.

Dave buzzed his Admin Assistant, Agnes, and asked her to come in to his office. Agnes had been with him since he acquired the company. Agnes was nearly 60 years old and was perfect for Dave. She was tall, thin, and quite competent, but she was not attractive (and that is being kind). Agnes Jablonski was also an American of Polish descent. She lived in Irving Park in the Polskie Wille, the landmark Villa District and historically known as the "Polish Kenilworth."

"Agnes," said Dave, "let's quickly review my travel plans."

"Great," she said. "I can't begin to tell how happy we all are that you are going to take four weeks away from work, and I am particularly happy that you are going to stay in Lublin. I have visited Lublin not too many years ago. You will enjoy the area and the history of Lublin, especially the Jewish heritage. Through the centuries, Lublin has been a great example of tolerance of the Jews. You will be staying at the Vanilla Hotel on Krakowskie Przedmiescie, which is nearly at the city center."

"Yes, Agnes," said Dave. "And you told me that if I didn't like it, there are other hotels in the area that I could switch and stay."

"True, but the Krakowskie Przedmiescie street is the heart of the area. Krakowskie Przedmiescie has many coffee shops and is at the heart of social gatherings and entertainment for visitors and the town's inhabitants. You are booked on an American flight to Warsaw, and we have a rental car for you to drive to Lublin—that will give you the opportunity to see some of the Polish countryside."

"Sounds like you have everything covered, as usual. I will call you from time to time to see how things are going."

"Don't call too often—you need this break and a time to relax and unwind. Everything will be fine here—you have good people working for you."

Dave was tired from the trip and was pleased to pull into the Vanilla Hotel drive. He was warmly greeted by the attendant, who parked his car and took his luggage. It was early afternoon, but he needed some shut eye. He decided he would start his exploration of Lublin in the morning. But he was hungry and wanted a drink before trying to sleep. The hotel attendant suggested the bar in the hotel—he could get a cold or hot plate and a nice glass of good Polish vodka.

Dave looked out the window of his room onto the streets of the Podzamcze district of Lublin. The streets were filled with people milling around looking at the foods, especially the desserts. He had been told that the place of residence of the Jews was an intellectual center of Jewish culture. From 1580, the main Jewish legation of the First Republic of Poland and the Rabbi, the seer of Lublin and the originator of Hasidic mysticism, lived here. During the era of the Reformation, Calvinist and Anan temples were located next to the Catholic parish. The religious debates were resolved in a spirit of tolerance and science; the religious wars, which haunted Europe, bypassed Lublin. As he scanned the crowds, he thought the populace resembled a typical group of people one would find in the

Polish sectors of his native Chicago. In a short time, he had become attracted to the area and its people. He felt at ease and at home here.

He decided he would leave the task of unpacking till later—he wanted to eat and have a drink before tackling the chore of unpacking. He left his room and ambled down the mahogany stairs to the hotel bar. The bar was small—he guessed about 2500 square feet. He was greeted with a warm hello from the bartender, who introduced himself as Stan. In addition to the bar itself, there were eight four-top tables and four two-tops. The bar was about half full with an equal mix of men and women, mostly middle-aged. Stan waved him to a spot at the end of the bar. He had a clear view of the bar. The plate glass window had "Bar Haven" encrypted in large old English letters and sat atop a "welcome" sign. Seated two stools down was a very attractive woman. He guessed that she was in her late thirties or early forties. He made a wager with himself that he would find out.

Stan asked him what he would like. Dave said, "I'll take a glass of local vodka, on ice, and a small Polish sausage plate."

"Yes, sir, I recommend our 'Lublin Vodka'—it's about as local as you can get." He shouted out the Polish sausage plate to the kitchen.

Dave took a sip of the vodka and rolled it around in his mouth before swallowing it. "Stan," he said, "this is excellent vodka—thanks for the recommendation."

"I wouldn't steer you wrong, my American-Polish friend," said Stan. "We like to have our American-Polish friends visit us. He chuckled, "There are more Poles in Chicago than there are in Warsaw. I would wager that you might know some of my friends and relatives who now live in Chicago. I think the same would apply to New York. I think from time to time that maybe I would move to the States, but, quite frankly, I love it here. We have the best of both worlds."

Stan motioned at the woman sitting two stools down from Dave. "She isn't a Pole from Poland or America—she isn't even Polish. She's a reasonably new customer. She lives in Lublin and works at the university. Let me introduce you. Hafsa, this is Dave Nogalski. Dave is from Chicago and is an American-Pole on vacation and staying here in Lublin."

She smiled at Dave, displaying a set of good-looking white teeth. Stan offered to buy them a drink, which Dave quickly accepted and which, after some hesitation, Hafsa accepted. He poured her a glass of Chardonnay and refilled Dave's vodka glass.

The more he looked at her, the more he liked. She had jet black hair cut to her shoulders, an olive Mediterranean complexion, and dark brown eyes. Her looks excited him. He wanted to see more.

"So, Mr. Nogalski, how long do you plan to stay in Poland and the Lublin area?"

"I plan to stay four weeks, given that my business doesn't require me to return earlier."

She smiled and said, "Let's hope that doesn't happen."

Dave returned the smile and said, "I do, too—I really want to see Lublin, and I need some time away from the job. Have you lived in Lublin a long time?"

"I've been familiar with Lublin since I was a young woman studying at the university in England. I fell in love with Lublin from the first time I visited, and I decided that someday, I would, God willing, come back and make Lublin my home." Hafsa was attracted to this American and saw no need to tell him everything, at least not yet. She saw no need to tell him that she had been in a marriage arranged by her parents. She lived in Lublin, but he spent only three months or so each year in Lublin. It was very recently that she became aware that he was not an international businessman named Allawi but a Palestinian terrorist by the name of Abu Awami. She was shocked that it took her so long to put all the clues together, but the clues had always been there. It wasn't until she overheard his telephone conversations with his underling, Sami, and had conversations with her cousins in Palestine that she was able to put the clues, information, and intercepts together. Also, he was a drunkard who drank until he passed out and who talked in his sleep.

Dave sipped the vodka and watched her do the same. The more he saw and smelled her, the more he was becoming enchanted with her. He knew he didn't have much time—four weeks would speed by quickly. He was tired and needed a little shuteye but wanted to see her again, and soon.

"Hafsa, would you like to have dinner with me tonight? You pick the place."

She didn't need much time to think this over—she immediately agreed. "Yes, that would be fine. I'd love to have dinner with you tonight. I know a number of restaurants that I think you would like. I'll come by here and meet you at, say, seven o'clock."

"Sounds great—I'll be here."

"Good. I have to get back to the university now—see you at seven."

Dave told Stan to close the bill and thanked him for his service. Stan knew he would be back and talked to him about Hafsa. "She's a beauty; she is also very knowledgeable about Lublin and its history. Did you know that the city's Jewish population was annihilated by the Nazis in World War II? Now, the city's Jewish population is being re-established. The Polish people suffered from countless invasions, not just by the Nazis, but also by Russo-Ukrainian invasions. Ask Hafsa about the Jewish presence in Lublin. She is an expert—that's her area of study and teaching at the university."

Dave went up to his room and had the sleep that his body needed. He slept fitfully and dreamed, mostly about her. His alarm went off at 6:00 p.m., and he shaved and showered to get ready for tonight. He was both excited and concerned about tonight's encounter. It wasn't that he hadn't seen other women since his dear Mary left this world, but here he was, in a foreign land, about to have dinner with a woman who had immediately excited him. He wondered if it was only a dinner or if anything would further develop. Thinking of Hafsa brought an intimate wave of pleasure to him.

She took her time walking back to her office. She always enjoyed the streets of Lublin, the merchants displaying their wares, the people, and, mostly, the tourists bustling among the attractions of Lublin's Old Town. To her, the excitement presented by Lublin would never cease. As she walked, she thought about the man she had just met this afternoon. The fact that he was an American businessman was a plus. American men of his class had a very good reputation when it came to their treatment of women. She couldn't help going back to that night when she told Abu Awami that their marriage arrangement was finished. He exploded when she told him she was divorcing him, but he had no say in this matter. He had told her that he was leaving and going to Brussels. She knew she would never see him again. He never knew of her investments in Brussels.

Fortunately, she had secured a large dowry and her uncle in Brussels had invested the money wisely, so she had no financial worries. That investment, plus her salary at the university, put her in reasonable financial shape. Her girls were students at a private girls' school in the Lublin area, so they were secure. Thinking back, she was sure that the arranged marriage suited Abu Awami's purposes just fine. She had followed her parents' wishes and traditions and had entered into the relationship—she was a dutiful daughter and respected her parents' wishes as a dutiful Palestinian daughter should. She immediately saw the irony of the situation in Lublin. Abu Awami was a terrorist whose only purpose in life was to eliminate Israelis in the hopes that the Palestinians would regain their rightful homeland. It was indeed more than ironic that his refuge in Poland was enabled by the Polish government's position of encouraging and working to rebuild a Jewish presence, as it had been over the centuries, especially in Lublin.

Truth was that she had always loathed Abu Awami, as he was short, balding, and not pleasant to look at or be with. His drinking had increased over time to the point that he was in a drunken stupor by early evening, and she didn't even have to resist his disgusting attempts to have sex with her. She wasn't sure how she would handle any questions that this Polish-American might have concerning her background, especially her marriage. He had to have known that she had recently divorced her husband, but she hadn't provided any details. She wondered if Stan knew about her marriage to Allawi al Otaibi and, if so, passed any information on to Dave. She quickly dismissed these thoughts—this was only a dinner with a Polish-American who would be in Lublin only for a matter of weeks. Just enjoy the moment, she thought. She began to think about where she should suggest they have dinner. The choices weren't infinite, but they were enough. She thought the Krakowskie Przedmiescie had several good restaurants and was one of Lublin's most frequented areas.

Abu Awami was now on a plane from Warsaw to Brussels. Sami had told him that, according to Maria deBellefroid, Kim David was en route to Brussels to see Milledufleur Rose. Abu Awami was excited about the prospect of eliminating the number two Mossad agent and his Brussels agent. Sami had arranged for Abu operatives to meet at a safe spot in Brussels. He was sure that the deadly encounter would be soon. This would be a great advance for the true Palestinian cause.

Abu Awami's flight into Brussels arrived on time. As he cleared Customs and Immigration, Sami was there to meet him. He greeted his leader with the usual male Arabic effusive hugs and kisses on both sides of the cheek. "Sami, what have you arranged for our meeting place?"

"We will meet at the Chez Leon. I've reserved a room for dinner and our meeting, just like the last time. All of our important people will be there. You can stay with me until we finish with David and Rose."

They took a taxi from Sami's place to Chez Leon. The owners of Chez Leon warmly greeted them, anticipating yet another very profitable evening—maybe, it would be more than one.

Abu Awami instructed the owner that they were not to be disturbed and to keep the drinks coming. The organization's people had already gathered and were awaiting the arrival of Abu Awami and Sami. Allawi al Otaibi greeted the assembly. "The plan is straightforward and simple. We don't have a specific time yet, but it should be a matter of days. We will have our people monitor the El Al arrivals from Tel Aviv. We will also have our people keep a watch on Ms. Rose's office at the University of Brussels. Our main attention will, however, be focused on her flat at 25 Rue Gerard. This is where we believe they will spend their, shall I say, last intimate moments on this earth, Inshallah."

"How about the local police, the UN police, the US FBI Legal Attaché, and NATO? He could be a problem."

Allawi looked to Sami and asked, "What about the FBI Legal Attaché, Sami?"

"We've been watching him closely," said Sami. "We do know that Gilmartin does have an extensive file on our operations, prepared largely by Tom Turner, Gilmartin's predecessor. Maria has entrapped Mike Burdick and has advised that Gilmartin refuses to share any information with Milledufleur Rose."

"But that could change," said Fahd Awami.

"Anything can change, Fahd, but we don't think any changes will stop us. It's a matter of days, not weeks."

"To recap," said Allawi, "we will kill them at Ms. Rose's flat. I personally will be there to shoot them—she will be shot first, just to increase the suffering of that Jew."

"Let's drink to that and the beginning of the end of the Jew occupying our country of Palestine," shouted Allawi.

Hafsa arrived at Dave's hotel promptly at 7:00. He was waiting for her in the lobby. They greeted each other with a quick embrace. She thought he looked great—he was neatly dressed in a beige sport coat with matching trousers and a dark red tie.

"My God, Hafsa, you look wonderful, even better than I remember," he muttered.

"Dave, I am recommending a restaurant called 'Le Autre Saison.' It is owned by an émigré from Quebec, Omar LaRoche. It's been quite popular with the natives and the tourists. The entrees are delicious, and the wine selection is superb," she said.

"Sounds good. Do they have Polish Vodka?" asked Dave.

"But, of course, mon amour," said Hafsa.

This had its desired effect on Dave, who noticeably perked up.

Hafsa took his hand and led him out of the hotel to the street where the populace was in a definite festive mood. She gripped his hand tighter and nudged her leg into his leg. His mood was brightened as he strolled with her. Her perfume had its desired effect. He hadn't felt this way in quite some time.

They continued ambling toward Le Autre Saison. When they arrived, Omar warmly greeted them and ushered them to a table for two at the rear of the perpendicular-shaped dining room. The lighting amply accentuated the walls, which were adorned with scenes of dancers from the Moulin Rouge. The restaurant was more than half-full, even at this early hour for dining in Lublin. The noise level was perfect for Dave—loud enough to allow for a private conversation but low enough to allow for individual table occupants to converse.

Dave was seated in a position where he could observe most of the customers of Le Autre Saison. Nearly all the patrons were middle-aged, except for the men sitting at two tables, who were in their fifties or even early sixties. Their companions were in their late twenties or early thirties and wore outfits that emphasized their shapely bodies. Not gaudy, but hardly the attire of middle-aged wives. Dave wondered if prostitution was legal in Lublin or just condoned. He thought of asking Hafsa, but he decided it was not pertinent, and he did not want to have Hafsa think he was possibly not au courant in the ways of the world. He did wonder if the couples were local Polish or Polish-American visitors. The women weren't particularly attractive, which led him to believe that they were Polish, either local or from America. He felt comfortable asking this question because Hafsa was not Polish and was much better looking than almost all of the women in the restaurant.

"Hafsa, I am curious—are the women here locals or from the U.S.?"

Hafsa looked at Dave, suppressed a smile, and replied, "What do you think? Do they look like the Polish women in Chicago, or do you think they are locals? How about the men—do you think they are locals or visitors from the States? You can forget about the young, scantily-dressed ladies—they are definitely le femme de nuit."

"I don't know, but my guess is about half are locals and the balance Americans, probably Polish-Americans. Am I right?" asked Dave.

"I'm not sure why you care—you are with me. But my experience tells me that about half are Polish-Americans with their wives and that the other half are local Poles with their wives or girlfriends, so your guess is close. But, once again, why do you care? You are with me, and I am not even close to being Polish."

"You are right—why don't we have a drink and you tell me about the menu?"

"That is perfect," replied Hafsa. She summoned their waiter, who appeared instantly.

"Good evening. My name is Jacques. What would be your pleasure?"

Hafsa gave Jacques a warm smile, engaged him with her eyes, and said, "I will have a glass of your finest Polish vodka, and make it a double. My companion will have the same, but make his a single—he may have some more work to do tonight."

At that, Dave thought he might have a miasma. He wondered if she was teasing or was seducing him.

All Dave knew was he hadn't been this excited by a woman in a very long time. He could hardly wait for the main course and dessert, whatever that might be. Hafsa recommended that he have the filet mignon, rare. She followed suit, commenting that, to her, "rare" was well-done.

As they sat at their table, she scooted closer and put her hand under his napkin, gently massaging him. Dave would have skipped the meal if he had the option, which he didn't—she was in control, and he would accept whatever transpired. He was just hoping it would be soon.

Jacques brought their steaks promptly, and Dave devoured his quickly. "Either you must have been starving, or you can't wait to get to the dessert," she smiled. "I will savor mine—good things are worth the wait."

She ate her entrée slowly, uttering a few "ah's" as she proceeded to finish the filet. "That was delicious, don't you agree, mon amour?"

Dave was beyond his ability to rationally engage in any coherent conversation. He could only wonder what he had fallen into and who the hell this woman was.

"Dave," she said. "Let's skip the dessert here and walk to chez moi, where I can provide you a dessert that you may not have had before but that you will love and never forget. I doubt if you have ever had anything close to it."

Dave was beyond coherence by now and could only think with one part of his anatomy. "I will do whatever you suggest."

As they ambled along to her apartment, she began asking him more questions about himself. She told him she just wanted to get to know him better. As they continued, she asked him if he had any more questions about her. He thought that there were many questions he had for her, especially about her recent divorce and how she managed to come to Lublin. He was sure he was in over his head, but he didn't care. He had led a prescribed life without deviating or even having fun. The word "fun" hadn't been in his vocabulary.

As they walked, she touched on her background and tried to explain the Palestinian mores and customs, which likely were completely foreign and inexplicable to him. The ways and happenings of the Middle East were foreign to those who had no exposure to an area light years away from the modern American way of life. Only a very small number of Americans had visited the Middle East or would even want to visit.

They arrived at her flat, where she escorted him up a flight of stairs. She led him into her place, which was comprised mostly of desert scenes and paintings of the pyramids and the Sphinx.

"Make yourself comfortable—here, I'll fix you a drink," she winked at him. "Remember, you will need to exert some effort this evening. Wait here and sip the drink, and I'll slip into something more comfortable. It won't be long. I'm anticipating a robust effort on your part, and I will do my best to help you."

Dave sipped the vodka and examined the art she had on the walls. He wondered about the authenticity of the art; he thought it was attractive but didn't have a clue. He would ask her about that—it would give him an opening for some conversation and a chance to ask questions about her. He heard a phone ring and her muffled reply. From what he could make out, he thought she had said, "I'll be there as soon as I can, possibly tomorrow night." He then heard her mutter, "Zut!"

She took the stairs down to the room in which Dave had been waiting. He watched her approach the settee in which he was seated. He gasped, "My God" as he gazed at her. She had on a gown that did little to cover her nakedness—in his mind, it just accentuated it. He couldn't suppress the inflammation rising in his groin. She snuggled up next to him, kissing him on both sides of his cheeks before she thrust her tongue into his waiting mouth. She then untied the gown, stood up, and let the garment fall to the floor. He could only gasp in pleasure. She then unbuttoned his shirt, undid his belt, took off his shoes and socks, and took his manhood into her hand. He was sure he wouldn't be able to suppress a climax, but, somehow, he did.

Hafsa said, "Now you can show me how much you want me. I know I want you—I need you now!" She straddled him and took him into her as they both mounted a frenzied attack on each other. They were in a mutual frenzy as they moaned and kissed until they released in a climax. She then kissed him again and again until he felt himself rising again. She then pulled him on top and began to have him inside of her. This time it was slower but with more intensity. He didn't know how long it lasted but was sure he had never experienced anything close to this.

Dave said, "Hafsa, I don't know what to say—I'm not even sure I know where I am. You are just fantastic! I don't want to leave you—can I take you with me?"

Hafsa put her head on his chest. "Dave, you have me spinning. I'm not sure we will be able to repeat this, but let's give it a try. Let me get up and bring you a glass of water—you'll need to replace the liquid you have lost." She rose and tied her gown before she padded to the fridge and poured a glass of water. She brought it to him and watched as he drained the glass.

She sat next to him and held his hand. "Dave, you said you would be here for four weeks and this is just day one, so you have nearly four weeks before you have to return to Chicago. But, unfortunately, I will have to leave Lublin and go to Brussels. I told you about my uncle in Brussels who has invested my money in property there. He called and told me that I will have to go there. He said he needs to review the investment portfolio. There are some changes that he believes we should make to the portfolio, and he insists that I review them with him. Also, he wants to show me property that he thinks I should acquire. He has booked me into the Conrad Hotel in Brussels. It may take two or three days."

Dave was less than pleased to hear the news. He didn't want to be away from her for hours, much less than for two to three days. "Hafsa," he said, "I don't want to be away from you for even a second, much less for three days. I think I'm falling in love with you. No, hell, I am in love with you. I don't need a building to fall on me to show me that. I just hope that you could return the feeling, at least a little bit."

Hafsa looked intently at Dave. She squeezed his hand. "Dave, I haven't felt this way, maybe only in my dreams. That you told me you love me makes me so happy that I think I could fly."

She then said, "I don't want to be away from you either. I have an idea. Why don't you come with me to Brussels? I can book your flight, and you won't need to get a room. You will like the Conrad."

He was beaming. "Great idea. I just will have to tell my office where I will be, and that's that. Are you sure your uncle won't mind?"

"He will like you—you are his type, and you will get along well together. Who knows—maybe you will invest in Brussels."

CHAPTER 16

"RENDEZVOUS IN BRUSSELS"

Hafsa and Dave Nogalski arrived at the Conrad after an uneventful flight from Warsaw to Brussels. As they were checking in, Hafsa caught a fleeting glance of a man walking with two other men. She gasped, thinking that he could be her now ex-husband, but she quickly rejected the thought. Why would he be in Brussels at the Conrad Hotel? Dave reacted to her noticeable gasp. "You look like you've seen a ghost," said Dave.

"Maybe I have, or maybe my imagination has run amok," replied Hafsa.

"What, or who, do you think you saw?" said Dave.

"I didn't get a good look, but that man could have been my now ex-husband. But why would he be at the Conrad or in Brussels?" she asked. She then remembered that, when she broke the marriage, he shouted that he was going to Brussels. Perhaps he was here because his number one underling, Sami, lived in the Brussels area. She quickly dismissed the thought as impertinent to her visit to see her uncle, Younnis.

The hotel's porter took their luggage and led them to their suite in the hotel. Room 620 was a large suite with a view of Avenue Louise. The staff at the Conrad furnished their room with a bottle of champagne and a welcome card. "You must be a good customer for the hotel to put a bottle of good champagne in the room," said Dave.

"I think it was because of my uncle—he is a big investor in the Conrad," said Hafsa.

"Well," said Dave, "why don't we sample the champagne? It's still early. When will you, or we, see your uncle?"

"That's a good idea," said Hafsa. "Are you going to try to get me in the mood to take off my clothes so you can have your way with me?"

Dave smiled as he said, "Sounds like a plan."

"Let me call my uncle and let him know that we are here."

Hafsa picked up the phone on the room's desk and called her uncle. She spoke French to her uncle. Dave waited for her to finish her call. She said, "Tout a l'heure."

"So," said Dave, "what's the deal?"

"He is coming over to the hotel. He said we have been invited to a party tonight."

Dave asked, "What time is he coming, and what's the party all about?"

Hafsa shook her head before she said, "He said he would be here at seven o'clock. The party is being hosted by Milledufleur Rose, a visiting Professor of Oriental and African Studies at the University of Brussels. He said he was invited because he is a big contributor to the university. He is also close to Bernard Lewis, one of the most prominent scholars on the Middle East. Lewis is a Jew, and so is Ms. Rose.

"There are a total of nine people who will be at the party. Four are Americans, including you. Ms. Rose is a British citizen. One of the women works for the University—she is a citizen of Belgium named Kirsten Rutten. Michael Gilmartin is an American who is a FBI legal attaché assigned to the EU, the EEC, Nato and Belgium.

His uncle is a retired FBI agent who is now a partner at a St. Louis law firm and who is very close to Michael. My uncle said he was a late addition to the party. One of the invitees is an American who has business ties to Saudi Arabia and spends some time there."

"Sounds like a pretty diverse crowd. Is the party at the Conrad?"

"No, it will be at a restaurant called 'La Quincaillerie,' which is 'the hardware store' in French. It is just a few blocks from here."

"So," said Dave, "we have time for a little champagne and recreation."

Hafsa shook her head and smiled. "You have a one-track mind, but I love the track."

She put her arms around him and hugged him before she began to kiss him and take him into her. "We have time, no hurry."

Milly and Kirsten continued their conversation, which centered on how they could convince Michael Gilmartin to share the file on the Palestinian terrorist organization that Gilmartin's predecessor had prepared over five years.

"Kirsten, we don't have much time before the guests for Jack Gallagher's party will be arriving. And we have some last minute additions to the guest list."

"Oh," said Kirsten, "who are the additions?"

"The President of the University called me and told me that he had invited a big benefactor of the University, a Christian Palestinian named Younnis Awwad, who resides in Brussels, his niece, Hafsa Awwad, and her new paramour, a Dave Nogalski, who is an American from Chicago and is on vacation in Lublin, Hafsa Awwad's place of residence."

"He must be a very big benefactor of the school for the President to invite him to a party you are throwing for Gilmartin's uncle. I don't understand how these Palestinians and the Palestinians' American friend fit in."

"Here is how they fit in—Mr. Awwad has a very large investment in Brussels's real estate, including the university. He also is the trustee for his niece's investment portfolio. The President thinks this may be a good opportunity to further cement the relationship with the Awwads. Hafsa has a very significant portfolio that her uncle controls," explained Milledufleur.

"This does complicate your objective to have Michael share his file with you. What are you going to trade with the FBI?"

"Something they don't have, or, at least, I think they don't have," said Milly.

Kirsten furrowed her brow as if to ask, "What is that?"

"I am almost certain they don't know of Mike Burdick's exposure to Fahd al-Otabi, the leader of the most dangerous of the Palestinian Terrorist organizations. When Burdick was in Saudi Arabia, he undertook a deal with a Saudi by the name of Ghanem al-Ghanem. This Saudi has a contract with Getty Oil to transport some of its excess crude to small refiners in the Partitioned Neutral Zone in Kuwait."

Kirsten asked, "How do you know this?"

"Because Mike Burdick told me. Michael Gilmartin talked to his uncle about the party and told him that Burdick was invited. This was no big deal, as Jack Gallagher and Mike Burdick are old pals. When they were talking, Burdick told Jack Gallagher that he was going to bring a local Belgian woman by the name of Maria deBellefroid to the party. Gallagher and Burdick somehow got to know this Maria and a friend of hers. Burdick latched onto this Maria and told Gallagher he was going to bring her to the party that

I'm putting on for Gilmartin's uncle. Jack Gallagher told Burdick that he had better clear that with me. So Burdick called and we talked."

"So?" asked Kirsten.

"Burdick gave me quite a story about Maria. Based upon what he told me, it could be that this Maria is also a punchboard for a local thug by the name of Sami, who is an underling of the Allawi al Otaibi terrorist group. He may know what they are up to here in Brussels. I'm sure Michael doesn't have this information. That's the trade."

"Sounds possible. I'll help you with Michael and his uncle as I said I would. This could be fun and, who knows, maybe I can have some fun with Jack Gallagher."

"I'm sure you could," said Milledufleur.

As she and Kirsten were talking about the "trade of information" with Michael Gilmartin, she thought back to the phone call she received that morning from Kim David. Kim had told her that he would be arriving on an early flight from Tel Aviv. He knew she was having a party that night for Gilmartin's uncle. He once again stressed how important it was to get the FBI file on the Palestinian terrorist gang. She asked him if he wanted to stay at her flat on Rue Gerard, but he declined and told her he would take a room at the Conrad. He indicated that he wouldn't go to the party—he insisted that she use the party to get the FBI file. He reminded her that obtaining the file was her assignment—they had to stop the Palestinian terrorist attacks. He told her he would see her after she had secured the file from Gilmartin. She knew Kim David expected no less than complete success. This only strengthened her determination to not only secure the information, but also to eliminate this Palestinian terrorist killing group from this earth.

The Palestinian terrorist gang had been checking the arriving flights from Tel Aviv. They didn't think Kim David would be using his name, but they did find out that four of the passengers were staying at the Conrad, one of whom had to be Kim David. From Maria deBellefroid, they knew that Milledufleur Rose was having a party for Jack Gallagher. It would be logical for David to go to the party. Their surveillance of Milledufleur's Rue Gerard flat showed no sign of David, but they figured that, given the time constraints, David had gone to the Conrad. They also reasoned that he might even be at the party. That would be perfect for their plans—they would be at the party. Sami checked the security at the Quincaillerie—he found none but suspected there could be a Mossad presence. If Kim David did attend, he and Milledufleur Rose would be the only two Mossad attendees. The Palestinian terrorist gang reasoned they had the edge in firepower.

Milly and Kirsten finished their discussion about the trade. "Let's get in position to greet our guests," said Milly. "I'll grab Michael, you take Jack Gallagher, and then we'll present our grand bargain and press Michael for the swap. It should be fun, but what happens after that may not be fun."

Milly led Kirsten to the table where she and Kirsten would sit next to Michael Gilmartin and Jack Gallagher. Fortunately, there were enough seats to accommodate the late additions of Younnis Awwad, his niece, Hafsa, and her male companion, Dave Nogalski. Milly would have Mike Burdick sit to her right. She would have Maria deBellefroid next to Burdick.

Kirsten asked Milledufleur, "One more time—why is it so important that you have access to the FBI file that Michael Gilmartin has in his safekeeping?"

"I don't know what the FBI file has that we don't have in our file, but I am here as the visiting Professor of Middle Eastern Studies. I would like to extend my stay for at least another year, and the more information I have, the better the odds are that my stay will be extended. I don't want to return to London—at least, not yet. I've told you about Drew Cahill, and he will still be in London. It is an untidy situation. One more year in Brussels would alleviate that problem. Not that he will or would cause a problem—it's just that it could be uncomfortable. Besides, I think there are more 'male hunting' opportunities here, and I could stop making myself available for Michael Gilmartin who, quite frankly, is becoming a bore to me, if you follow my drift."

"So, you think that you would be able to impress the President and other key faculty members with your knowledge and information on the Middle East, especially the Israeli/Palestinian ongoing conflict?"

"That's a pretty good summary."

Kirsten gave Milly a knowing smile and tilt of the head. "Well, Michael is a good-looking young man—if his uncle has a similar appearance, I will do what I can to help, including using my body sexually. It's been a long dry spell for me, and I would look forward to having intimate sexual contact. In other words, I need to get laid."

Milly was thinking that if it weren't for the urgent need to eliminate this Palestinian threat, this could be a good opportunity to have some interesting sexual adventures. She had never met Mike Burdick, but, based on his reputation, he just could be a fun encounter. Didn't someone—probably Michael—tell her that some of his acquaintances labeled him with the moniker of "Mr. Fun?" Maybe he could be fun. She interrupted this brief reverie and told herself that the elimination of the Palestinian terrorist gang was of critical importance. She had the disquieting feeling that the conflict would reach its climax soon, very soon.

The visibility afforded by the layout was excellent. With their position on the second floor, they could see any entrant through the front door, the only entrance to the building. As she and Kirsten were looking down at the first floor, they saw Michael Gilmartin walk in with a man who could only have been Jack Gallagher. Kirsten nudged Milly and muttered, "If that's Jack Gallagher, he better have iron pants on, or else he's in for a big ride tonight—my big ride."

Milly chuckled. "One small step for mankind but a giant step for your plans."

As they bantered, Mike Burdick entered with Maria deBellefroid. Milly smiled to herself, thinking that this Maria doesn't have a clue that she has set up a trade for the FBI file. She thought that this Maria looked like "punchboard"—too much makeup, too tight, and gaudy dress. She guessed that Burdick wasn't interested in class, just ass.

A few minutes later, Dave Nogalski walked in with a Mediterranean beauty, Hafsa Awwad, and a dignified-looking gentleman, Younnis Awwad.

The entourage entered the Quincaillerie and ascended the staircase one by one. Milledufleur greeted Michael Gilmartin cheerily. She then put her arms around Jack Gallagher and pressed Kirsten into him, saying, "This is my fellow member of the University of Brussels, Kirsten Rutten. She will be your dinner companion tonight. She is very knowledgeable about the interaction of Belgium and the Middle East, especially Palestine and Israel."

Milly then extended her hand to Mike Burdick, ignoring Maria. "I am Milledufleur Rose. From what Michael Gilmartin has told

me, you have strong business connections in Saudi Arabia and
Kuwait. We all look forward to hearing about your experiences
there, especially about your exposure to the Palestinian terrorist
group, Abu Awami."

"I guess your source is Michael Gilmartin, who has picked up
this information from Jack Gallagher."

"Quite right," said Milly.

Kim David was pacing in his room, putting the pieces of this
puzzle together, and finally came to a logical conclusion. He called
Milly on her cell phone and laid out the scenario to her. He told her
that, based on the information the Mossad had recently uncovered,
they expected a move by the Abu Awami gang soon, possibly tonight,
maybe at the dinner party. He emphasized that securing the FBI file
was critical and that there wasn't much time. He questioned her
about that and if she thought Gilmartin would have the file with
him tonight. Milly was reasonably sure that he would, as he would
be with his uncle before the dinner. She was sure that he would
discuss the possible trade of information with his uncle. He told her
that, based on the intelligence the Mossad had, they were sure that
the Palestinian terrorist gang would come to the Quincaillerie. Kim
was sure that he would be the target for assassination and that Milly
would be the bait. Milly wasn't shocked by this revelation—she told
Kim David that she was prepared and that she would get the file.
Kim assured her that the Mossad had the situation under control.

After all the guests had been seated, Yvonne greeted them and
announced that she would be serving them tonight. "I'll start with
your drink orders and will then take your choices for dinner. The
guest of honor is Mr. Gallagher, so I'll begin with him and his

dinner companion, Ms. Rutten." They both ordered wine, she a Chardonnay and he a Cabernet. Milly and Michael followed suit. She then took orders from the rest of the group.

Milly snuggled up to Michael, and Kirsten took Jack Gallagher's arm in hers. "Jack," said Kirsten, "I'll skip to the chase, as you Americans would say. As the visiting Professor of Middle East Studies, Milly has files on Palestinian terrorist groups, particularly the Abu Awami group. She is anxious to have her contract extended for another year. We know the FBI legal attaché has an extensive file on this group. She is prepared to allow the FBI to review her file in return for Michael's office allowing her to peruse their file. We believe we have information that the FBI doesn't have and probably vice versa. We both have an incentive to bring this terrorist group to justice.

"As a member of the University's faculty, and as a friend of Ms. Rose, I ask that you trade this information. I will privately give you the information we don't believe you have." While talking, Kirsten was gently massaging Jack's leg and whispering into his ear. Jack replied, "Let's have a look."

Milly gave them the file she had on Maria deBellefroid and her lover Sami. This was information they didn't have. Jack persuaded his nephew to let Milly review their file. Milly quickly discovered that the FBI file documented Abu Awami's stays in Poland for three months in Lublin and that he was married to Hafsa Awwad. They knew he spent time in Poland but didn't know where in Poland. This cemented the trade.

Milly called Kim and gave him the news. He smiled broadly and told Milly that they were ready. The party went on, and Milly prepared for the expected arrival of Abu Awami gang. Milly took the vodka bottles and laced them with Dioxin. She told Yvonne that they expected some "party crashers" and that she should put those bottles away for their uninvited guests.

The decibel level began to rise as the guests imbibed and ate. Meanwhile, four swarthy-looking men—Abu Awami, Sami, and two others—entered the ground floor of the Quincaillerie. As they entered, they were surrounded by eight Mossad agents, who disarmed the gang and told them to proceed up the stairs. While watching, Mike Burdick gasped and uttered, "Holy shit."

Milly asked Yvonne to prepare the special vodka drinks for their new arrivals. Milly raised her glass to the new arrivals and uttered a toast and welcomed them to hell. They drank heartily, and the Mossad agents led them stumbling down the stairs and into cabs headed toward the Chez Leon. Maria ran out, leaving Mike Burdick alone. Milly sat next to him and told him that they had a lot to talk about.

Jack Gallagher asked Kirsten, "What was that all about?"

Kirsten said, "I'm not sure, but let's just enjoy the rest of the night."

Burdick looked at Milly sitting next to him and asked her what she had meant when she said they had a lot to talk about. She smiled and took his hand. "Now that you have rid yourself of that tramp, Maria, I don't want you to be lonely. You will still be spending time in Kuwait and Saudi Arabia."

"Yes, that will go on for a few more years."

"On your returns, you can still stop in Brussels," Milly suggested.

"Sure—what did you have in mind?"

"I'd like to get to know you better," Milly replied.

Burdick smiled and told her that they could start tonight.